The Girl
Across the Way

(Original title: The Cat Across the Way)

by ANN HUSTON

Illustrated by John Fernie

SCHOLASTIC BOOK SERVICES

NEW YORK · TORONTO · LONDON · AUCKLAND · SYDNEY

Text copyright © 1968 by Anne Huston. Illustrations copyright © 1970 by Scholastic Magazines, Inc. This edition is published by Scholastic Book Services, a division of Scholastic Magazines, Inc., by arrangement with The Seabury Press, Inc., publishers of the book under the title THE CAT ACROSS THE WAY.

1st printing .... November 1970

Printed in the U. S. A.

FOR MY NIECES AND NEPHEWS
Garth, Holly, Abby, Jimmy, David,
Tommy, Timmy, Drew, and Ann Elizabeth

WITH SPECIAL THANKS TO
Dr. Howard Barth
Barbara Terry Bell
Mary Jane Carlson
Lyn, Jimmy, and Tommy Checkelsky
W. Richard Connelly
Mary Gulmi
Arlyn, Carl, Jane, and Russell Huston
Donald Ruch

1

MONDAY MORNING . . . ugh! Lacey made a face at the pink walls, then got out of bed and walked over to her window. Maybe it had all been a bad dream. Maybe when she looked out she would see their own backyard where the marigolds were in bloom, and the garden where she and her father had picked ripe tomatoes just a week ago, and the garage where her pony, Tiny Joe, was bedded.

But it hadn't been a dream; it was real. They had moved to the city, and the view from her third-floor window proved it.

Just below was the black-topped parking lot, where her father and all the tenants in the apartment building parked their cars. Beyond the lot, on the other side of a high chain-link fence, was a dirt yard and a one-story, flat-roofed brick building that partly hid a big gray house. And beyond the house were other houses just like it and more apartment buildings like hers — all crowded so closely together it was hard to tell where one stopped and another started.

Lacey's vision blurred as she looked at the unfamiliar Cleveland skyline. She knew that she should be getting dressed, but she didn't want to think about school . . . not yet. Still in her pajamas, she pushed aside a pink curtain and climbed onto the windowsill to sit, letting her legs dangle over the edge. The black wrought-iron balcony outside her window made her feel secure — almost as if she were sitting on their porch back home in Three Corners.

With the sun out the September air was warm, yet the thought of the coming day made Lacey feel cold. To push it away, she searched the fenced-off dirt yard beyond the parking lot for the yellow cat.

Lacey had first noticed the cat last Thursday

morning when they were moving into the apartment. He was lying curled up asleep on the roof of the brick building, and she had been glad just to know that there was an animal nearby. Later that same day she had seen him playing in the yard, wildly dashing up and down an old ladder propped against the end of the building. She had laughed and laughed at the big cat's crazy antics; so every day since then, she had been watching him.

Suddenly she spotted the cat by the fence on the near side of the yard. He was stalking a stray piece of newspaper as though he were a hungry tiger stalking an antelope. Oblivious of the cars pulling out of the parking lot, he crept toward the paper on his stomach, his long plumey tail twitching from side to side as he moved.

Lacey smiled. He looked so silly creeping along that way, acting as though he were completely hidden under thick jungle grasses when he was really in plain sight of everybody.

Just as the cat leaped high and landed ferociously on the helpless piece of paper, Lacey heard her mother call in a high, soft singing way: "Lacey? You dressed? Breakfast in five minutes, please?"

On school mornings back home Lacey had always loved to hear her mother's call to breakfast, the sound was so cheery. But today she didn't feel a bit cheered. The call was only one more reminder that she would soon have to face her first day in a new school.

She swung her legs onto the windowsill, but kept her head turned outward. "I'm watching the yellow cat, Mother," she called.

"No time for that cat this morning, Lace." Now it was her father peering at her from the open bathroom window which also looked onto the little balcony. The lower half of his face was covered with shaving lather. It made his eyes, as blue as Lacey's, seem even more blue. "School today, Hey! Hey!" he said and winked.

"I know, Daddy. I only wanted to watch for a little while," Lacey said, giving up and crawling back into her bedroom.

Hey! Hey! She wished she could feel as cheerful about the new school as her father did about his new job. But, of course, for her father it wasn't a new job by now. He had already been working at it for three weeks.

He had come to Cleveland the third weekend in August to start as the new route supervisor with the baking company. Labor Day weekend he drove back to Three Corners to tell Lacey and her mother that he had finally found them a place to live, and they had moved to the city on the following Thursday.

Lacey sighed. Just four days ago. It had all happened so fast! And already her mother and father seemed to feel at home. But Lacey didn't feel at home at all. She didn't like the apartment they had moved into, she didn't like the street they lived on, and she was sure she wouldn't like the school she had to go to.

The apartment was small — just a living room, a kitchen, a bedroom, and a bathroom; the street was noisy; and the school was a huge, ugly place that looked like a scary castle . . . a castle with creepy dim stairwells, long winding halls, and unfriendly, leering faces.

Lacey thought of all those unfriendly faces and wished that she were back home in Three Corners. If she were, she'd be *hurrying* to get dressed. There would be Tiny Joe to feed and water before school, then her best friend, Pam, to meet at the railroad crossing.

Tiny Joe. She didn't want to think about the pony. Now he was tied in *Pam's* barn, nickering at Pam, who at this very minute was probably feeding him his morning grain and hay. Now he was Pam's, not hers. All she had was a crazy yellow cat that slept on someone else's roof, a cat she couldn't even call by name . . . just an animal to look at from across the way.

"Lacey, please hurry!"

Her mother's voice brought Lacey's attention back to getting dressed. She decided to put on her favorite blue dress, one that matched her eyes and always made her feel special. She needed something to make her feel special today.

Brushing the snarls out of her short blond hair, she hurried from her bedroom and bumped into her father as he was coming out of the bathroom. She couldn't sidestep; there wasn't enough room. To get to the kitchen both of them had to squeeze past unpacked cardboard boxes piled one on top of another in the hallway.

Lacey's mother was in the living room making up the sofa bed. Since Lacey had the only bedroom, her parents slept in the living room on a brown sofa bed her father had bought secondhand. Lacey didn't like the sofa bed. It wasn't nearly as comfortable to sit on as the old maroon couch they had left behind.

Everything seemed out of place and strange in this smaller kitchen, even the familiar green kitchen table. Sitting down next to her father, Lacey began to sip her orange juice slowly. Her father drank his in four swallows.

"Want me to go with you to school again, Lace?" he asked as he set down his empty juice glass. "This is the only morning this month that I don't have to be downtown at six-thirty."

Lacey thought of the looks she had gotten when she had walked into the fifth-grade classroom with her father on Friday afternoon. "No, thanks, Daddy," she said, pouring cornflakes into her bowl even though she didn't feel hungry. "I'll go by myself."

"Okay. Say! We're going to sample a new coffee cake this morning at the product meeting. Want me to bring you a piece?"

Lacey shook her head. In Three Corners it used to be fun to sample the new items that the Superb Baking Company put out for her father to sell on his bakery route. But it didn't sound like fun this morning.

"Aw, come on, Lace," her father said, reaching out to rumple her hair. "Don't look so unhappy. You're going to do fine, today. Just remember: the kids in the new school are no different from the kids in Three Corners — only the faces are different."

Lacey looked at her father intently. "I hope so, Daddy. But I know I'd rather be seeing the faces in Three Corners."

Lacey's mother came in from the living room, a kerchief tied over her own blond hair. "No more talking, you two. Eat! It's late and I want you out of here so I can get to work," she said, smiling at both of them.

Lacey and her father finished breakfast quickly and were soon ready to leave.

"Have a good day, Stan," Lacey's mother said, standing on tiptoe to kiss him. Then she gave Lacey a gentle hug. "I'll bake you a chocolate cake with your favorite fudge-marshmallow frosting for supper, dear. And you'll both be surprised to see how many more cartons I get unpacked by evening."

"Oh, Mother," Lacey burst out, "don't unpack anything. Maybe something will happen and the bakery will give Daddy back his old job in Three Corners."

Lacey felt her mother's arms go tightly around her. "Lacey, we've been all through this before. Daddy's old job doesn't exist any more so we *can't* go back. Cleveland is our home now."

"But I don't want to live here, Mother," Lacey said, almost shouting. "I want to live in Three Corners!"

The uncomfortable silence that followed and the troubled faces of her parents caused Lacey to regret her words almost immediately. All three had made a solemn promise not to talk about Three Corners. They had agreed that it would only make them remember and that remembering would only make them sad. And now Lacey had broken that promise.

"We'll talk about this at supper, Lace," her father said softly, ending the silence. "Now we'd better go, or I'll be late for my meeting and you'll be late for school." Taking her by the hand, he led her through the living room and out of the apartment.

As they walked down the stairs, neither said anything about her outburst. When they reached the ground floor they separated, her father going out the rear door to the parking lot and Lacey hurrying out the front door.

Their apartment building stood on the corner of Woodhill and Lascana, and since the parking lot exit was on Lascana, her father would soon be driving past. Lacey ran to the corner. When she saw the old black Plymouth pull out of the lot she raised her arm. Her father answered with a loud honk of the horn as the car came toward her.

He had the green light so he didn't stop, but he honked the horn again and waved. Lacey waved back as she watched the car turn left onto Woodhill and disappear in the rush of traffic. She kept on waving even though she knew he couldn't see her any more.

Then, with a growing feeling of dread, she turned and started in the opposite direction for the school.

2

LACEY had three long blocks to walk. To keep her mind off the huge stone school building ahead, she went slowly and looked in every store window along the way.

She passed a candy store, a drugstore, a jewelry store, two dime stores, a clothing store, a supermarket, and a bank. They were all new to her. So was the constant noise and rush of traffic going north and south on Woodhill. In Three Corners she never passed a single store on the way to school. And the mornings were so quiet that she could hear the wrens scolding long after she had left her house.

No wren could be heard on this street, though. No wren would even want to live here, Lacey thought, looking up. The sun was shining but an eye-stinging haze hung between it and the ground, blocking the brightness and carrying with it the acrid smell of oil from the refineries in the flats. Lacey shook her head. She still couldn't believe that this place was going to be her home.

At last she reached the intersection of Kinsman and Woodhill just before the school. Over the noise of the traffic she could hear the kids on the playground yelling at each other. Lacey stiffened. She wished now that her father had come with her. But he hadn't, so she would have to face it by herself.

As she crossed the street and drew closer to the four-story school building, she stared in amazement. The playground was jammed with kids — more kids on one playground than she had ever seen before. There were so many that there wasn't any room left to play. And all of them were standing in lines, some stretching clear across the black-top to the fenced-off area where the teachers' cars were parked.

From the talk with her teacher on Friday, Lacey remembered that she, too, had to get in line. Something else different! They never lined up in Three Corners. But here, because there were so many children, there had to be order, her new teacher had told her. So in good weather the children lined up outside until the doors were opened.

Lacey didn't know which of the doors led to her own fifth grade. She glanced around the playground in an effort to locate her teacher, but the great mob of kids, yelling and crowding each other, made it impossible for Lacey to spot her.

Just then the twenty-to-nine bell rang. The seven sets of doors around the back and sides of the school were opened from the inside, and the children began to push through them.

"Are you in the fifth grade?" Lacey asked a boy in a nearby line.

"No, stupid, the sixth grade," the boy said and walked away.

Lacey ran to another line. "Are you in the fifth grade?" she asked a girl.

"Which one?"

Lacey stared. Was there more than one fifth grade? She hadn't thought of that. What was her teacher's name? Then she remembered. "Klein," she shouted in relief. "Klein. Mrs. Klein's. Room 106, Corridor B."

"Well, I'm not deaf," said the girl. "And I'm not in Mrs. Klein's room. I'm in Mrs. Dorsey's. We're on the fourth floor, Room 408, Corridor M. Hey! You'll make me late!" she yelled and ran from Lacey to catch up with her line, which was just disappearing through one set of doors.

Lacey spun around. She had to find her own class! If she went into that gigantic place by herself, she knew she would never find her way. She ran to a third line and tugged at the shirt sleeve of a boy near the end. "Are you in Mrs. Klein's fifth-grade class?" she asked breathlessly.

The boy looked at her for a moment without answering. "You a new kid?" he said finally.

"Yes," Lacey said. "Please tell me. Are you in Mrs. Klein's fifth grade?"

The boy grinned. "Yeah, sure. I'm in her room."

"Oh, thank you," Lacey said. "Then I'll just follow you."

"Yeah, you do that," said the boy, laughing loudly.

Lacey quickly looked down at herself to see what was so funny, but she could see nothing unusual — her slip didn't show; no dirt on her dress. She left the boy, took her place at the end of the line, and began to move inside with the others, greatly relieved that she had found someone in her class in time.

The line she was in marched down a long corridor, turned right into a shorter one, and at the end of it started up a flight of stairs. As Lacey took the first step, she tried to remember if she and her father had climbed stairs on Friday to get to her class-room. She didn't think they had. But the boy who had said he was in Mrs. Klein's room was still in line ahead of her, so she knew she must be going the right way. Maybe they were all going to the auditorium for a special program this morning. That would be fun!

Feeling safe now, Lacey glanced around as she walked. The floors of the school were wooden, the stairs metal. The corridors and stairwells were two-toned: the bottom half green and the top half cream.

Green and cream. Green and cream. She chanted it softly as she climbed each step. There was so much noise she knew no one would hear her. And the funny rhyming sounds helped to keep her spirits up.

Green and cream. Green and cream. Lacey was the last to reach the second floor, so she had to hurry to catch up with the line as it turned from the main hall into a side corridor. But when she rounded the corner she knew something was wrong. They were not going to the auditorium, they were going to a classroom. The teacher standing outside of that room was not Mrs. Klein. And the number on the door was not 106.

"Room 106, Corridor B." Lacey whispered the directions. "106. 106." Then it came to her. Room 106 was on the first floor! She had been right about the steps after all. Now she knew why the boy had laughed. He had lied to her and she had believed him.

"Hello. Are you a new sixth grader?" asked the teacher at the door.

"No," said Lacey, feeling the fear begin to grow again. "I belong to Mrs. Klein's fifth grade. Room 106, Corridor B."

"Then you're on the wrong floor," the teacher said. "Your room is on the first floor and on the other side of the building. You'd better hurry or you'll be late."

"I don't know how to get there," Lacey blurted out.

Just then the nine o'clock bell rang, and Lacey jumped. She was sure she must have been standing directly underneath it, it seemed so loud.

"Go to the Principal's office," the teacher said as she stepped inside and closed the door on her noisy class. "They'll tell you."

Lacey stood alone in the now quiet hall. Go to the Principal's office, the teacher had said. But how could she? She didn't know where *that* was either! A tiny sting of pain shot across the bridge of her nose as tears gathered. She quickly pressed her hands against her eyes. She wasn't going to cry — she was going to find her room.

Hurrying back the way she had come, along the main corridor and down the stairs, she went to the first floor and began to search for Corridor B. The tardy bell rang — five after nine. Lacey frowned. Now she *was* going to be late. And latecomers always got stared at, especially if they were newcomers too.

She found Corridor C and followed it, thinking it would lead to Corridor B. Instead it led to Corridor A. Not knowing what else to do, Lacey began to walk even faster down that corridor, hoping to find her room before someone discovered her wandering through the halls. She read the numbers on the doors. 123 . . . 121 . . . 119 . . . they were getting lower, so she must be getting closer. She broke into a run, then stopped short. Corridor A dead-ended at doors to the playground.

Frantic now, Lacey pushed open one of the doors and went down the steps onto the playground to start all over. That sixth-grade teacher had said her room was on the other side of the building. So she ran past the huge black fire escape to a door on the opposite side of the school.

When she went to open it, she saw it had no handles. She tried to tug it open with her fingers but couldn't. Giving up, she tried a second door, then a third and a fourth. But none had handles. She was locked out!

The sting of pain returned, only this time Lacey

was powerless to stop it. She sat down on the step below the handleless doors and began to cry.

After a few minutes she became aware of a voice nearby, a gentle voice, not talking to her, but talking steadily to someone. Lacey scrambled to her feet, hurriedly wiped her eyes and tried to brush dry the wet spots on the front of her dress. Then she walked backward toward the playground, looking all the while at the school in an effort to discover where the voice was coming from.

Just to the left of the doors where she had been sitting was a row of open windows. Inside them a class was in session. A teacher was standing at the head of the class, talking. It must have been the teacher's voice she had heard.

Lacey ran to the windows intending to ask for help. But once she drew near, she realized that she was too short to reach them. The only thing she could think to do was to gather herself together, jump straight into the air, and hope that someone would see her face at the window.

The first time she didn't jump high enough to even reach the window. But on the second jump she caught the eye of a tall boy standing by the pencil sharpener. Lacey took a deep breath and gathered herself together for a third leap. At the top of her jump, she squeezed out the word "Help" to the boy at the sharpener. Then he disappeared as her feet hit the ground again.

Below the window, Lacey listened carefully. The teacher's voice had stopped, and now in its place she could hear what sounded like a boy's voice.

She jumped again to see what was happening. This time all eyes were turned toward her, and when she appeared the class burst out laughing. She didn't jump again, but stood and waited. Now, at least, they knew she was out there.

Soon heads were poking out the window to stare at her. Then the teacher's head came out the window too. Lacey gasped. It was Mrs. Klein, her own fifth-grade teacher.

"What are you doing out there?" asked the teacher kindly.

"I got lost," Lacey said, trying to cover up the shaky sound in her voice. "I went through a door and it locked. I couldn't get back in anywhere. All the doors are locked."

Some of the boys and girls who had stuck their heads out with the teacher giggled.

"What grade are you in?" Mrs. Klein said, raising a hand to the others for quiet.

"Fifth grade," Lacey said, feeling her face flush from the stares she was getting.

"Which one, do you know?"

"Yours. Don't you remember? My father brought me in on Friday."

The teacher looked at her for a moment. "Oh, yes," she said finally. "You are Lacey Lewis from Three Corners. The new girl who is starting a week late. Stay there, Lacey. I'll send someone for you."

To Lacey it seemed as if the whole class had gathered at the windows. Some of the boys were making faces at her. A few of the girls were whispering. She wondered if the tear spots on her dress had dried yet, but she didn't dare look down to see. That would call attention to them. Instead, she turned her back on the staring faces while she waited for the someone Mrs. Klein was sending.

Soon one of the nearby doors opened and a plump girl with long, black hair stuck her head out. "I'm Rosette DiNalli," she said. "I've been sent to rescue you." Then she giggled.

Lacey felt her face flush again. She was aware of her own plain blond hair cut very short to keep it out of her eyes when riding Tiny Joe. Was that what the girl was giggling about? Or was it because Lacey had gotten locked out?

"It's not funny, you know," Lacey said as she walked into the school again through the door Rosette was holding open.

"Oh, I'm not laughing at you. You must have felt just awful standing out there. But it was funny when

Willie Thompson told us there was a face at the window. Then you popped into sight, and you looked so fierce that Willie said you must be an angry dwarf. You know, like Grumpy in *Snow White!*" Rosette sputtered with laughter again as she led Lacey down the green and cream hallway.

Lacey didn't think it was funny at all, but she didn't say so to Rosette. She was just glad to follow her to the classroom. When they walked in, the entire class cheered. Rosette bowed low and dragged Lacey down in a bow too. The class laughed and clapped their hands.

Lacey jerked free of Rosette's grasp and straightened up. She was sure they were making fun of her. "It's not polite to laugh at someone in trouble," she said angrily. "I didn't know the doors would lock. In my school back home they don't."

From the rear of the room came a loud voice. "Three cheers for Grumpy!" It was the boy, Willie Thompson, who had seen her at the window.

With that Mrs. Klein rapped loudly on her desk. "Quiet! Quiet, please, everyone!" Then, after the class had quieted down, she continued. "Lacey Lewis is right. It isn't polite to laugh at someone in trouble, especially a newcomer who doesn't understand city schools. Lacey is from the country where schools are small and where doors don't have to be locked against strangers coming uninvited into the building.

Here, Lacey, such a practice is necessary. In the future, remember that the main entrance, the one that faces Woodhill Road, is always open and patrolled. You may always come in that way."

Lacey nodded, hoping the teacher would let her take her seat. She could feel everyone's eyes staring at her and she didn't like it.

"Now, class, let's give Lacey a proper welcome. Then we can get on with our work."

"Welcome to Lester Maywood School, Lacey," the class chanted.

"Thank you, class," Mrs. Klein said. "You may take your seat, Lacey. There in the second row, the fourth seat back."

Lacey hurried to the empty seat. It was right across from the girl with the long black hair, Rosette DiNalli. Lacey stuffed her lunch in her desk. Without looking around, she took a piece of paper out of her notebook to try to work the problems on the blackboard.

But she couldn't do them. They blurred and the blackboard blurred. Putting down her pencil, Lacey folded her arms across her desk, laid her head on them, and shut her eyes as tight as she could.

3

A LITTLE LATER, when she felt more at ease and while everyone else was still busy doing mathematics, Lacey lifted her head to look around the room. On the wall over the front blackboard was a big clock; in a vase on Mrs. Klein's desk was a bouquet of marigolds; and at the back of the room by the coat closet was a reading corner. A nice room, Lacey thought. But it couldn't compare with her old classroom in Three Corners.

She looked at the boys and girls and wondered if she would ever get to know all their names. Rosette DiNalli was hunched over in the next row, squirming in her seat and chewing on her pencil. Lacey smiled to herself. That was just the way Pam did when she was working problems. Pam wasn't very good in mathematics.

Thinking about Pam reminded Lacey of Tiny Joe again. They couldn't bring the pony with them to the city, so Pam's father had bought him. Pam loved animals almost as much as Lacey did. She had promised to take good care of Tiny Joe and to write every day and tell Lacey how he was. So far, though, she hadn't written at all. Lacey hoped there would be a letter in the mail today.

The sound of a chair scraping the floor brought Lacey back to the classroom. Mrs. Klein got up from her desk and stood in front of the class. She was a plain-looking lady, Lacey decided, but she had a nice smile and that helped.

"Boys and girls," the teacher said, "I know it's only September, but I want you to start thinking about Thanksgiving. In November all the fifth grades are going to give a Thanksgiving Day program. Since we are in charge of the decorations for the auditorium and the stage, I thought we might talk about it now. Does anyone have any ideas?"

Lacey's hand was the first one up. At home she

was always the first to have ideas, and usually the class liked and used them.

"Yes, Lacey?"

"In Three Corners," Lacey began, "some of us brought in corn shocks. We got them from farmers who lived nearby. We stacked them in the corners of the room and then we got—"

Lacey stopped abruptly. Willie Thompson had said something that made the boys near him laugh. Lacey hadn't heard what he had said, but she was sure it had been about her.

Mrs. Klein silenced the boys. "Would someone please tell me and the rest of the class what was so funny? Lacey made a perfectly good suggestion."

"Whoever heard of getting shocks from corn!" Willie Thompson said in a loud voice. "All I ever get a shock from is a light socket."

The whole class burst out laughing then. All but Lacey. She sat stiffly in her seat, eyes fixed on the teacher.

Mrs. Klein rapped on her desk. "Very funny, Willie," she said, with a stern look toward the tall boy.

But Lacey was not fooled. She knew Mrs. Klein had thought it really was funny. She had seen the teacher smile, then quickly cover it with a frown.

"Very funny, indeed," Mrs. Klein went on, "but Lacey was not talking about electricity. She was talking about dried stalks of corn which farmers have in their fields in autumn. Isn't that right?"

Lacey nodded dumbly.

"Thank you, Lacey. Perhaps if someone goes for a trip to the country, they can bring us some corn shocks. Any other ideas?"

Other hands went up and other ideas were voiced. But Lacey didn't listen; she didn't care how they decorated the auditorium. Never had anyone made fun of one of her ideas before. She looked at the clock on the wall. Only an hour had gone by. How could she stand being in this class all day long? She wondered if three o'clock would ever come.

To her surprise she got away sooner than she had expected. There was no cafeteria in Lester Maywood School, and even though Lacey had brought her lunch, she had to carry it back home at noon to eat it.

Lacey was so glad to be outside that she ran the entire three blocks to their apartment building. She climbed the stairs too fast, tripped, and bruised her shin. Everything was going wrong today! By the time she reached their door Lacey felt she would burst.

She knocked loudly. When her mother opened the door, Lacey plunged breathlessly through it. She wrapped her arms around her mother's waist and cried right there in the open doorway.

The afternoon at school was no better, and at the supper table that evening Lacey told her father everything that had happened. "Please, Daddy, can't we go home?" she pleaded. "Can't we go back to Three Corners?"

Before answering, Lacey's father looked at her for a moment, serious frown lines etched across his forehead. "Lacey," he said in a firm but gentle voice, "Mother and I know how lonely you feel away from your friends and Tiny Joe. But we can't go back. You know that Superb was forced to close its branch in Three Corners because it was losing business. Home service just can't compete with the supermarkets and the discount houses any more."

Lacey toyed with the food on her plate, almost sensing what her father was going to say next and not wanting to hear it.

"I'm just lucky the company thought enough of me to offer me the promotion to route supervisor here in Cleveland. You know, Lace, they could have just as easily let me go. Then I wouldn't have had any job. And jobs are hard to find these days, especially good ones."

Her father paused for a moment; then, when Lacey didn't look up, he continued. "I tried working at the pickle factory, Lace. I tried it because you didn't want to move. But I couldn't make enough money there. And, Lace, you know I wasn't happy. A man has got to be happy in his work. It's very important. Do you understand?"

Lacey didn't answer. She was remembering the week her father had worked nights packing pickles in the factory, that week in August before he went to Cleveland. Night shift was all he could get.

It had been a horrible week for all three of them. The only time she saw her father was at three-thirty in the afternoon as he was leaving for the factory. And then he had always seemed tired or grumpy.

At the end of that week, he had called Lacey to him. He told her he missed the fresh air, the sunshine, and his customers waiting for their fresh bread or jelly doughnuts. He just couldn't work at the pickle factory, he said; it made him too unhappy. And Lacey knew that was the truth because her mother had confessed to her that for a week her father hadn't smiled once or even hummed while he was shaving.

So her father had accepted the promotion. And here they were. Now it was Lacey who was unhappy.

"Do you understand, Lacey?" her father asked again. "Do you see why we can't go back?"

"Yes, I see," Lacey said at last, knowing there was no other way to answer.

"Then please give yourself time. You'll find friends and soon you'll forget all about Three Corners."

"No, I won't, Daddy," Lacey said solemnly. "I won't ever forget."

Lacey's mother rose from the table. "You don't have to forget your old friends, Lacey," she said as she took off the supper plates. "They're part of your life. But don't shut yourself off from making new friends, too."

Lacey's father leaned over and gave her a kiss on the forehead. "Mother's right. Try, Lacey. Please?"

Lacey nodded.

"Now," said her father, "let's have some of that delicious chocolate cake with the gooey frosting that Mother made. I bet it tastes better than any cake Superb ever baked."

But Lacey wasn't hungry any more. She asked to be excused and went to her room, wanting to be by herself. She got into her pajamas and robe and crawled onto the windowsill. To her dismay, the cat wasn't in sight. But the evening air was still warm, and there was still plenty of light, so she stayed out there anyway, hoping he would soon appear. She wanted to laugh, to forget about the day at school and about the even worse disappointment afterward — no letter from Pam.

A flock of pigeons caught her attention. She watched them soar and wheel and glide above the tops of the buildings. They seemed so free, not a part of the city at all. She wished she could join them.

Then a loud miaow drew her attention back to the roof of the one-story building. There the cat was, walking on the very edge, daring himself to lose his balance and plummet to the ground below. She didn't know who owned the fenced-in plot around the building, but whoever it was hadn't planted any bushes or grass to cushion the cat if he did fall.

He made it to the old ladder without a slip and backed down it at a reckless speed. Once on the ground, he raced to the chain-link fence across the yard. Then, testing cautiously for a paw-hold, he started to climb it.

"You crazy cat, you can't climb that!" Lacey warned. "It's too high. Besides, how are you going to get over the barbed wire at the top?"

Three strands of barbed wire rose above the fence. Once they must all have been taut, Lacey thought, but now some were loose and twisted together. A menace either way to anything or anybody trying to get over them.

At last the cat reached the top of the chain-link. Was he going to try to climb the barbed wire? Yes! He stretched his right paw over his head, gingerly searching for a hold between barbs. He found a place and tightened his claws around it, then did the same with his left paw. His body swayed slightly as he lifted a hind leg and searched for a bracing point.

Lacey held her breath. She had never seen a cat try anything like this before.

As soon as all four paws were on different strands of the loosely strung wire, Lacey knew the cat was in trouble. He bobbed crazily when he tried to stretch upward; the same thing happened when he tried to ease a hind leg back to the main fence. He was trapped, high off the ground and balancing on loose strands of treacherous barbed wire like a tightrope walker.

Lacey groaned. She wanted to help him but there was nothing she could do.

4

THEN she saw the cat move. In slow motion, stalking
the wire below him as he had the paper, he eased a
searching hind paw downward. At times Lacey
wasn't sure he was really moving, it took him so long
to stretch that leg out.

But at last he had the paw on solid support. Then
he had the other one secure. He eased himself down
until his front paws were on the chain-link too. With

that, he was out of danger, and he backed down the main fence until he was once more on the ground.

Lacey saw him shake a forepaw violently. It must have gotten torn on one of the barbs. She saw him lick it several times and was sure that was what had happened. Then he disappeared behind the building, limping slightly.

Lacey uncrossed her fingers and breathed deeply, feeling trembly inside and suddenly very tired. She crawled through the window, took off her bathrobe, and got into bed. Then she did what she had done every night since leaving Three Corners: She picked up Tiny Joe's picture from the bedside table and talked to it.

"Oh, Tiny Joe, I wish I could see you again." She stroked the pony's neck with her finger. "I miss you so much."

A light knock on the door made her put her picture back on the table.

"Come in," she said.

"All ready for bed?" asked her father. "So soon?"

"Don't you want to take a bath tonight, dear? It would be nice and soothing." Her mother smiled warmly at her.

"No," Lacey said. "I just want to go to sleep."

"Well, good night then," said her mother, pulling up the top sheet.

"Everything will be fine, Lacey," her father said, giving her a kiss. "You'll see."

When they went out, Lacey picked up the picture again. "I hope they're right," she whispered. "Good night, Tiny Joe."

At school the next day Lacey kept to herself. No one spoke to her the whole time except Mrs. Klein and Rosette DiNalli.

Mrs. Klein said good morning when Lacey passed her desk to sharpen a pencil. Later, during mathematics, Rosette looked up from her squirming to ask: "How much is nine times fifteen?"

"One hundred and thirty-five," Lacey answered without hesitation.

Rosette whispered, "Thanks." And that was all.

That evening, her father asked her how the day had been.

"Only two people talked to me," Lacey told him.

"Did *you* talk to anyone?"

"No."

"No one will speak to you if you don't speak to them," her mother said.

"Everyone always spoke to me in Three Corners. And sometimes I didn't speak first."

"That's because they knew you, Lace," her father said. "They don't know you here. I admit, I think someone should come right up to you and say, 'Hi, I'm Patsy Popindoop. Why don't you come play with me?' But if they don't, you have to march right up and speak to them."

Lacey grinned at her father. "What should *I* say? 'Hi, I'm Lacey Lopindoop'?"

"Well," said her father, giving her nose a playful tweak, "I think Lacey Lewis might sound better!"

"I'll try," Lacey said finally. "Tomorrow, I'll try."

Lacey said good morning to Mrs. Klein and smiled at Rosette the following morning. Rosette stopped talking to little red-headed Betsy, the girl in front of her, and leaned across the aisle.

"How'd you know that answer so fast?" she demanded.

"What answer?" Lacey was on her guard immediately.

"Nine times fifteen?"

"Oh, that." Lacey laughed, relieved. "I like math and I just knew."

"You *like* math?" Rosette tapped Betsy. "You hear that?"

Betsy shook her head, and Rosette pointed to Lacey. "She likes mathematics!"

Lacey didn't know whether Rosette was making fun of her or admiring her. But she remembered her promise to try, so she just waited until she was sure which it was.

"You do?" Betsy stared at Lacey.

Lacey nodded. "Yes," she said evenly. "Next to horses, math is my favorite subject."

Lacey heard Rosette gasp. But the tardy bell rang before she could find out the reason for the gasp, and after the bell there was no more talking.

When the nine forty-five bell rang, Rosette leaned across the aisle again. Lacey noticed how much Rosette's hair looked like a horse's mane. She thought it was beautiful.

"Did you say you like horses?"

Lacey nodded. "More than anything."

"So do I!" Rosette exclaimed. "Hey! Why don't you come play jump rope with us during gym this morning?" She grabbed Lacey's hand, pulling her out of the room before Lacey even had a chance to speak.

Lacey smiled to herself. Rosette had used almost the same words her father thought "Patsy Popindoop" should say. It made her wonder — if he were right about a silly thing, maybe he was right about a serious thing like making friends.

Some of the fifth-grade girls were already gathered in a far corner of the playground jumping rope. Lacey felt a surge of excitement. She loved to jump rope. Back home she was one of the best and could jump double-dutch twenty-five times, if she had good turners.

"Hey, everyone!" shouted Rosette. "This is Lacey. She's going to jump with us. And she likes horses, too."

"Oh, no!" They all groaned and made faces. "Not another one."

"Oh, yes," said Rosette, "and we horse-lovers stick together, don't we?" She put an arm across Lacey's shoulder.

Lacey smiled. "Yes," she said, "we do."

"Well, why don't the horse-lovers take turns turning?" said Betsy. "I've been turning for hours."

"We've only been out here five minutes," Lacey said, remembering the time they had left the room.

"Never mind," Rosette said. "We'll turn. Come on, Lacey."

As long as the girls were jumping a single rope, Lacey didn't mind turning. She had to turn a long time, too, because all the girls were good single rope jumpers. When they started using two ropes for double-dutch, though, she found it hard to contain her eagerness to jump. She had to watch herself so she wouldn't turn badly and cause someone to miss.

But she didn't have long to wait with double-dutch. Mary, the third girl through, missed.

"Want to jump now, Lacey?" asked Rosette from the other end.

"Oh, yes," Lacey said.

"Lacey's going to try now," Rosette announced.

"But, Rosette, it should be your turn," Betsy said.

"Never mind. I give Lacey my turn."

"Thank you, Rosette," Lacey said, handing her ends to Mary.

Rosette and Mary began to turn, while Lacey stood ready. Then she saw her moment and leaped. A perfect entry!

"One . . . two . . . three . . . four . . . five . . . six . . . seven," the girls began to chant.

Lacey kept the rhythm of her jumps even, smooth, matched with the rhythm of the turners. She was doing fine.

"Eight . . . nine . . . ten . . . eleven . . . twelve." The girls chanted louder.

Lacey had to steady herself to keep from catching the excitement of the counters. These girls were impressed, she could tell. She was going to make a record; she was going to show them they had laughed at the wrong person.

"Thirteen . . . fourteen . . . fifteen. Hey! She beat Rosette's record!" they shouted. "Sixteen . . ." Now there was amazement in their counting. "Seventeen . . . eighteen . . . nineteen . . . twen —"

Suddenly one rope faltered and drooped slightly. Lacey jumped automatically, but she knew it was useless. The drooping rope had already caught on her shoulder.

"You missed!" the girls yelled.

A sinking feeling came over Lacey. She had hoped so much to make a record-breaking jump, but it had been ruined by one girl. Lacey wheeled to face the girl, Mary. "It was your fault," she said politely but firmly. "You didn't turn right."

Mary shrugged. "I'm sorry. But my arms got tired."

"Don't be nasty, Lacey," Rosette warned.

"I wasn't being nasty," Lacey protested. "I was just saying what was true. Because she didn't turn right, she ruined my jump. In Three Corners I've jumped as high as twenty-five with good turners."

"Don't brag."

"I wasn't bragging." Lacey couldn't figure out Rosette. Before she had been very friendly. But now she was making it look as though Lacey was a poor loser.

"Yes, you were," Rosette said stubbornly. "And you missed. So take the ropes and let me have a chance."

Lacey knew Rosette was right. No matter whose fault it was, she had missed and she should take her turn at the ropes again. Back home she would have. But here she couldn't — not after the bossy way Rosette had talked.

"No, I won't," Lacey said. "It wasn't my fault. I get another chance."

"No, you don't," Rosette said. "If you can't play the way we play, then you don't play at all."

"That's right," chimed the other girls. Then they all turned their backs on Lacey and started jumping rope again.

Lacey pretended not to care. But she walked quickly away so they couldn't see how disappointed she was. She turned only once to find out what they were doing. Rosette was still jumping double-dutch and the rest were cheering her on.

5

THE INCIDENT on the playground bothered Lacey. She hadn't been bragging. She had only been telling what was so. But Rosette had turned the whole thing around and that had made her angry. And her anger had made her be something she would never have been at home . . . a poor loser.

Lacey wondered what to do. She knew she should apologize, but she couldn't just stand up in class and say, "I'm sorry." That would only make everyone laugh. No, she'd have to start with Rosette and then get to the others. After all, Rosette had been the most friendly . . . at first.

"Horse-lovers stick together." Well, they certainly hadn't stuck together at recess, Lacey thought glumly. Then she remembered an idea that had worked once when she and Pam had had a fight. Taking out a piece of paper, she began to draw a picture of herself riding Tiny Joe. Beneath it she printed: TINY JOE SAYS TO TELL YOU LACEY IS SORRY. While Mrs. Klein was putting spelling words on the board, Lacey slipped the drawing onto Rosette's desk.

Rosette gave Lacey a quizzical look. Then she studied the drawing, wrote something on it and handed it back across the aisle.

She had written: WHO IS TINY JOE?

Lacey scrawled MY PONY in big letters on the back of the drawing and gave it to Rosette.

Rosette answered with: TELL HIM I'M SORRY, TOO. TALK TO YOU IN ART CLASS.

During art class that afternoon, Rosette cornered Lacey. "You have a pony?" she asked.

Lacey nodded. "I used to. But I had to sell him when we moved here."

"Bet you hated that."

"I did. I miss him a lot. I used to go riding every day after school."

"Every day! You were lucky. I've only been riding once in my whole life. What'd your pony look like?"

Lacey tried to describe Tiny Joe, but she couldn't, really. The only way for Rosette to know what he looked like was to see him or at least a picture of him. Lacey thought about her picture at home. She hesitated; after all, she didn't know Rosette very well. But the desire to share Tiny Joe with someone was too great. "Come home with me after school and I'll show you a picture of him," she said hurriedly.

"Okay," Rosette said.

There it was . . . that simple. The fight over the jump rope was forgotten and Rosette was coming to her house.

When the three o'clock bell rang, Lacey waited for Rosette instead of bolting out the door. Together they walked down Corridor B and out of the school. Suddenly Rosette stopped.

"Oh! I forgot," she said, frowning. "I can't come over today. I have to go right home to study math."

"But you said you'd come!" Lacey blurted out, disappointment surging through her. Ever since art class she had been thinking about Rosette's visit, making a list in her head of all the things she could tell Rosette about Tiny Joe. Now Rosette wasn't coming. She had to do something!

"I know I did," Rosette said, her voice cutting through Lacey's thoughts. "But I can't."

"Why not?"

"I told you. I have to study math. My mother said so."

"Come to my house," Lacey urged. "I'll help you with your homework."

"You will?"

Lacey sensed that Rosette was weakening. "Sure. You can call your mother from my house and ask her," she said quickly. "I'll tell you all about Tiny Joe, then we can study. Okay?"

Rosette grinned. "Okay," she said. "Let's go."

Together they walked toward Lacey's building. Lacey felt very light and bouncy. She even had an urge to skip, but caught herself just in time when she saw who was ahead of them.

Standing outside the candy store next to Lacey's building were Willie Thompson and some of the other boys from their class. They were sparring with each other.

"Hi, DiNalli," Willie called as Lacey and Rosette drew near.

"Hi, Thompson," Rosette answered. "What're you eating?"

"Popsicle." Willie looked at Lacey then and grinned wickedly. "Hi, Laceyeee," he said, dragging out the last part of her name and making it sound screechy.

"Hi, Willieeee," Lacey shrilled back, doing the same with his. She laughed at the surprised look on Willie's face when he realized his own name could be made to sound that way too.

"Ha, ha, Thompson," Rosette said. "She got you that time."

Lacey didn't wait for Willie to retaliate. She ran past the candy store and yelled for Rosette to follow. When she started for the front door of the apartment building she saw a look of amazement on Rosette's face. "What's the matter?" she asked.

"I didn't know you lived here," Rosette said. "I live on Lascana Street. We're practically neighbors."

Before Lacey could answer, she heard Willie Thompson shouting at them from the candy store. "Hey, Laceyeeee," he yelled, "bring me some corn shocks. I need my battery recharged."

Ignoring the shout, both girls hurried inside and up the stairs.

"That Willie Thompson!" Rosette said, tossing her head indignantly. "Sometimes I like him and sometimes I don't."

"What do you mean?" Lacey asked, not thinking about Willie, but wondering if her mother would be upset with her for bringing Rosette home without asking. But lots of times in Three Corners Pam had come home with her and it had been all right.

"Oh, sometimes he's very mean," Rosette said.

Lacey silently agreed, remembering how Willie had laughed at her for being lost and made the joke about her corn shock idea in class.

They reached the apartment door and Lacey knocked. As the door opened, Lacey caught a look of surprise in her mother's eyes, but she also saw a look of pleasure.

"Lacey, how nice!" her mother said, smiling. "You've brought a friend home from school."

Gratefully Lacey smiled back as she and Rosette stepped into the living room. "Mother, this is Rosette DiNalli. She likes horses too. She came to see the picture of Tiny Joe."

"Well, that's fine," said Lacey's mother, closing the apartment door. "You'll have to excuse us, Rosette. We're not all unpacked yet." She beckoned the girls to follow her to the kitchen. "You show her Tiny Joe, Lacey, and I'll get a little snack ready for you. By the way, something came for you in the mail today. It's on your bedside table."

Lacey raced to her bedroom. A green envelope lay on the table near Tiny Joe's picture. She looked at the return address. It was from Pam! "Hooray!" she shouted, running back to the kitchen where she suddenly realized she had left Rosette standing.

"It's from my friend, Pam," she told her excitedly. "She's the one who has Tiny Joe now." Lacey ripped open the envelope, took out the pages and began to read.

"Lacey, don't you think you should wait until your guest leaves?" her mother said.

"Oh, Mother," Lacey groaned, "I've waited so long to hear. Maybe I can read the parts about Tiny Joe to Rosette."

"That's okay," Rosette said. "I don't mind. I have to call my mother anyway, please."

Then Lacey remembered the math and her promise to help. She explained everything to her mother. Mrs. Lewis showed Rosette into the living room, and while Rosette telephoned home, Lacey eagerly read the letter from Pam.

When she had finished it, she ran into her bedroom and shut the door. There she reread it to make sure she hadn't skipped a page. She turned the green sheets of paper over and over, even searching the envelope for a possible missing page. But she soon realized that there was nothing missing. It was all there. The long-awaited letter from Pam . . . and it had just two sentences about Tiny Joe.

A wave of sickening anger swept Lacey. For an instant she felt like tearing the letter into tiny bits of green confetti. But instead she stuffed it under some clothes in a drawer in her dresser. Then she hurried back to the living room.

"Let's study out here," she said to Rosette who had finished her call. "It's nicer."

It wasn't the truth, but suddenly Lacey didn't want to study in her bedroom — not with the letter there.

Rosette shrugged. "Okay. What'd your friend have to say?"

"Oh, not much," Lacey said offhandedly as she seated herself on the sofa bed and opened her math book. "Just a bunch of stuff about a fair."

"Nothing about your pony?"

"Oh, sure. She says he's eating all the hay she feeds him. Look, Rosette, let's do our homework now. We can have cookies later. Okay?"

"But you haven't told me about your pony," Rosette said.

"Yes, I have."

"No, you haven't. You haven't even shown me his picture. You said in school you rode him every day. Where did you ride?"

Lacey looked up from the book. "We just went for rides, that's all. Up the dirt road and down. And sometimes through the woods. Let's do our homework."

"Not until I see his picture."

"Just a minute then." Lacey frowned and went to her bedroom for the picture of Tiny Joe. "Here he is," she said as she came back. She held out the picture just far enough for Rosette to see but not to touch.

"Hey! He *is* beautiful. No wonder it was hard to describe him."

"Now, let's study," Lacey said abruptly. She took the picture back to her room and shut the door. When she returned Rosette was seated on the sofa bed, an open book in her lap.

"I never had a pony," she said, looking up at Lacey, "but if I had, I'd sure have more to tell about him than you did."

For half an hour Lacey and Rosette worked on mathematics. Then Lacey's mother brought them cookies and milk. When they had finished the snack, Rosette got ready to go home.

"Thank you, Mrs. Lewis," she said. "I had a nice time. Thanks a lot for helping me, Lacey. Won't Mrs. Klein get a shock tomorrow when I know some answers? And I don't mean a corn shock!" Rosette giggled and left.

"What did Rosette mean by that, Lacey?" her mother asked.

Lacey sighed. "It was just that idea I had about corn shocks for decorations. I guess she thought it was funny, too."

Lacey felt her mother's gaze on her. "What's

wrong, Lacey? Did you and Rosette have a quarrel?"

Lacey shook her head and walked away, unable to answer her mother just then. She went into the living room and sat down.

"Lacey, what's wrong, dear? Was it Pam's letter? Did something happen to Tiny Joe? Is he hurt?"

Her mother sat down close beside her on the sofa bed and the nearness comforted Lacey. Keeping her eyes on the tufts of material on the sofa arm, she began to explain.

"Tiny Joe is all right, Mother, I guess. At least, Pam *says* he's fine and eating all the hay she feeds him." Lacey paused, almost unwilling to say what was troubling her. "But, Mother, that's *all* she says about him. Not one more word. The rest of the letter is about the ribbon she won at the fair last week with her 4-H sewing project. She promised to tell me about Tiny Joe, Mother, but she didn't. She's my best friend — why didn't she keep her promise?"

"I don't know, dear," her mother answered slowly, "unless Pam got so busy with the fair and school starting that she just forgot."

"How could she forget? I haven't."

"I can't answer that, Lacey. Sometimes we have friends who remember and sometimes friends who forget."

"Well, I'm a friend who remembers."

Lacey's mother hugged her. "Yes, you are, dear.

But maybe you should be one who forgets just a little. Then you'd have a happier time here."

Lacey stiffened. "How? How would I?"

"Oh, my!" Lacey's mother smiled. "Such a fierce look. I think you would be happier because you wouldn't be living in yesterday. You would be living in today. Do you understand what I mean?"

Lacey shook her head.

"One day you will. I liked your friend, Rosette."

"She's not my friend." Lacey got up from the sofa, uneasy about the things her mother had said. "She's just a girl who likes horses. She's bossy . . . and she exaggerates."

"Well, Lacey, we can't have everything," said her mother, getting up to go to the kitchen and start dinner.

At supper that night her father told all about his day at work, how he had found three new customers for one of the routes he was in charge of. Lacey was relieved he didn't ask her about her day. Pam's letter was left in the drawer, unshared, unmentioned.

Lacey talked to Tiny Joe a long time that night, remembering the rides they had taken together, the things they had seen. She felt so close to him that once she thought she heard him whinny. But when she listened more closely, she knew it was only the cat across the way yowling.

But all that remembering still didn't tell her what Tiny Joe was doing *now*, how he looked *now*. Oh, why hadn't Pam written more about him? Was she really taking good care of him or was she just letting him stay all alone in that musty barn of theirs? Maybe she wasn't even —

Lacey stopped herself. It wasn't fair to suspect her best friend of neglecting him. She closed her eyes tight to shut out all the troubling thoughts. As she drifted off to sleep she heard the yellow cat yowling again. It was a horrible noise, but a comforting one, too; at least the cat was close by.

6

BEFORE she left for school the next morning, Thursday, Lacey put the picture of Tiny Joe in her notebook. Hearing from Pam had made her feel more lonely than ever for her pony, and she wanted to be able to look at his picture during school. Having it along cheered her and made her feel a little mysterious, too, as though she were carrying a powerful secret force that would protect her from any harm.

When she got in line on the playground, she was surprised to have Betsy greet her. Even Mary turned around and said hello. Lacey felt giddy. Did the hidden picture really have some strange power over people? Then she saw Rosette farther up the line and knew that Rosette must have told them about coming to her house. Lacey hoped she hadn't mentioned Pam's letter.

They filed into their room in time to see Mrs. Klein writing on the board: MATHEMATICS HOMEWORK QUIZ. SHARPEN YOUR PENCILS.

Rosette was the first to return with her sharpened pencils. "Hi, Lacey," she said, smiling. "Guess what? I'm not scared of the quiz this morning, thanks to you."

Lacey smiled back. Rosette wasn't even thinking about that letter; she was only worried about the quiz. "It's a good thing, Rosette. Getting scared freezes your brain."

Rosette giggled. "It sure does."

As soon as Mrs. Klein had passed out the quiz papers and they could begin, Lacey looked over at Rosette. There was no squirming, just a fierce chewing on the pencil. Lacey was sure that was a good sign, and she bent to concentrate on her own paper.

After everyone was finished, Mrs. Klein had them exchange papers in order to mark them. Lacey got Rosette's paper and Rosette got Lacey's. Mrs. Klein began to call out the correct answers. When they were done, Lacey grinned as she handed Rosette's paper back to her.

Rosette let out a loud whoop. Everyone turned to look at her.

"What's all that noise for, Rosette?" asked Mrs. Klein.

"I got a hundred!" Rosette said proudly.

Willie Thompson cheered from the back of the room.

"Quiet, please, Willie!" Mrs. Klein said. "That's fine, Rosette. Who marked Rosette's paper?"

Lacey raised her hand.

"Thank you, Lacey," Mrs. Klein said. "Now, class, please pass your papers up. I would like to look them over. And while I'm doing that, I want you all to read Chapter Three in your geography books."

There was a rustle of papers, a slamming of desk tops as the boys and girls did what Mrs. Klein had requested. Soon the room was quiet again as everyone began to read to themselves.

Lacey had just finished the second page of the chapter when she heard Mrs. Klein softly call her name. She looked up. Mrs. Klein was motioning for her to come to the front. Puzzled, Lacey rose and walked up to the teacher's desk.

Quietly, in a voice that only the two could hear, Mrs. Klein said, "Lacey, I know you are good in mathematics, and that pleases me. Judging by your work so far, you are one of my top pupils. But because you are good you must not be tempted in a quiz to help others who are not so good. Do you know what I'm trying to say?"

Stunned that anyone would suspect her of doing something like that, Lacey was speechless.

"These homework quizzes," Mrs. Klein went on, "are only to help me find out who is learning what. They don't count toward a grade. Even so, I want to know what each student's correct score is, not what the changed score is. Now, Rosette got one hundred today. Is that really her correct score, Lacey?"

Rising anger brought back Lacey's speech. "I didn't change any of Rosette's answers," she said, feeling the sting of pain across her nose that meant tears. She fought to control them. "And it's mean of you to think I did."

"I'm sorry, Lacey, but I had to know," Mrs. Klein said gently. "Thank you. You may sit down now."

"What'd she want?" hissed Rosette when Lacey returned.

"She thought I cheated for you," Lacey mumbled, unable to look Rosette in the face.

"What?" Rosette screeched, waving her hand. "Mrs. Klein, Mrs. Klein," she called out, "may I speak to you?"

Mrs. Klein must have given Rosette permission because Lacey could hear her steps going up the aisle and then coming back after a few minutes.

"I told her," Rosette whispered. "I told her how you helped me study all afternoon yesterday. So I *knew* the answers. I didn't have to have anybody cheat for me!"

The sting gone now, Lacey looked up. "Thanks, Rosette," she said gratefully. "It really wasn't all afternoon, though."

Rosette grinned and stuck out her hand. "Who cares? We horse-lovers have to stick together, right?"

"Right," Lacey said, giving Rosette's hand a hard shake.

Then Mrs. Klein was standing beside her. "I want to apologize, Lacey," she said. "And I want to thank you for helping Rosette with her math. That was very generous of you."

Lacey didn't know what to say, so she just smiled. Mrs. Klein went back to her desk and started talking about geography. Rosette winked and shook her clenched hands in a victory sign. Lacey winked back and returned the sign.

Only once during the day did Lacey have a chance to look at Tiny Joe's picture. That was in the library. She and Rosette and Betsy were all at the same table reading. When she opened her notebook to sneak a look at the picture, Rosette saw her. And before Lacey could protest, Rosette snatched the picture away.

"See?" Rosette said to Betsy, waving the picture in Betsy's face. "Isn't her pony beautiful?"

"Please give it back, Rosette," Lacey said.

Rosette quickly handed it back. "Sorry, Lacey. I didn't mean to grab it away like that. I just wanted to show Betsy."

"That's okay," Lacey said, tucking the picture into her notebook again. "He is beautiful, isn't he?"

After school, Rosette asked once more to see the picture. Reluctantly Lacey gave it to her. Rosette immediately hugged it tightly to her heart, and Lacey had to stop herself from grabbing it away. She knew Rosette was only showing how much she liked the picture, but Rosette was much too rough with it. It was the only picture of Tiny Joe that Lacey had. There could never be a reprint because Pam had lost the negative.

As soon as Rosette handed it back, Lacey carefully put it away. Then they started walking home. They had just crossed Kinsman Road when Rosette groaned loudly.

"What's the matter?" Lacey asked.

"Forgot my history book," Rosette answered. "Go on. I'll catch up with you." And she ran back to school.

Lacey started on by herself. Every now and then she looked over her shoulder to see if Rosette was coming, but there was still no sign of her by the time Lacey reached her own block. Just ahead she saw the boys hanging around the candy store again. She steeled herself to pass them, expecting more taunts from Willie Thompson.

As she got closer she realized that they were not even looking in her direction. They were all watching something in the street between the parked cars. Willie Thompson had a broken broomstick and was poking at it. Lacey eased her way into the crowd and peered between the legs and arms to see what was there.

She gasped with horror and pity. A blood-spattered pigeon flopped convulsively against the curb. It was trying to right itself without the use of one wing, obviously broken. But each time it managed to get on its good side, Willie Thompson, with the broomstick for a prod, forced it onto its back again.

Lacey put her notebook on the sidewalk and lunged at Willie. "Stop it," she cried. "Stop torturing that poor pigeon!" She jerked the broomstick out of Willie's hand and threw it under the parked cars.

Willie grinned. "Well, if it isn't Laceyeee. What'd you throw away my broom for? I was just tickling this little ole bird with it."

"I saw what you were doing," Lacey said. "You weren't tickling, you were poking."

"Aw, who cares," Willie said, giving the bird a

nudge with his shoe. "It's just a dirty, filthy pigeon, full of diseases."

"I care," Lacey said, picking up the wounded pigeon. "It's an animal and it's hurt. Why don't you help it instead of hurting it?"

"Oh, mind your own business," piped one of the other boys. "It's going to die anyway."

"Yeah, mind your own business," Willie said, eyeing the bird in her hands. "And give me back my pigeon."

Lacey stiffened. They were beginning to crowd her. She tried to back away but felt herself hemmed in by the car parked behind her. With one hand she pressed the pigeon against her stomach. With the other she made a fist.

"You keep away from me," she shouted at them. "I'm not going to let you have this pigeon to torture any more. So just keep away!"

Trapped against the car and with only one hand to defend herself, she waited for them to jump her.

7

BUT WILLIE never jumped. Instead he turned to ward off blows he was getting from behind.

"Cut it out, Thompson," a voice shouted. "You leave her alone!"

Although Willie's height blocked Lacey's view, she knew the voice. It was Rosette's. Lacey didn't know when Rosette had arrived, but she was glad to have her there, and on her side.

Lacey took advantage of the distraction to get away from the car. The pigeon in her hands struggled feebly. She talked softly to it and tried to calm it.

"Aw, DiNalli, you spoiled our fun," Lacey heard Willie say.

"Some fun!" Rosette snapped. "Torturing a wounded bird and scaring a girl in your own class. Now go home or I'll tell my father."

Whoever Rosette's father was, the mere mention of him made the boys run.

"You sure scared 'em away," Lacey said in a shaky voice. "Thanks."

Rosette shrugged. "It's nothing. I'd have been here sooner, but Mrs. Klein asked me to help her clean the erasers."

"How'd you know it was me in trouble?"

"I heard you shouting, so I came running. I told you Willie is mean sometimes. Let's see the pigeon."

Gently Lacey handed the bird to Rosette. It wasn't struggling any more; it just lay in a rumpled heap in Rosette's hands. Rosette stared at its lidded eye. "It's dead," she said at last.

"Oh, no!" Lacey petted the pitiful still body.

"We can bury it at my house," Rosette suggested. "There's dirt in the back. Come on."

"I'd better tell my mother," Lacey said.

"You can call her from my house — the way I did at your house yesterday."

Lacey picked up her notebook and fell in step with Rosette. She knew her mother wouldn't mind, but she would call the minute she got to Rosette's.

They rounded the corner and headed down Lascana Street. They passed the black-topped parking lot where Lacey's father parked his car, then an empty store building. Just beyond the store building was a big gray house with a long front porch and two front doors, one at each end of the porch. Rosette turned up the walk on the left side of the house.

"This is where I live," she said. "On this side. Come on."

Lacey followed Rosette up the wooden porch steps. "We really *are* neighbors," she said, surprised to find that Rosette lived so close. "I've never seen you walking to school, though."

"I go the back way to meet Betsy," Rosette said, stopping on the porch to examine the pigeon once more.

"Why do you have two front doors?" Lacey asked.

"This is a double — a two-family side-by-side. We live on this side and the Querciolis live on that side. All these old houses on Lascana are like that. Come on in."

Lacey followed Rosette inside. Rosette's mother, a plump lady with hair as dark as Rosette's, met them in the living room. She looked sad when Rosette told what had happened with the pigeon.

"You were brave to protect the bird," she said to Lacey. "Those boys can be very cruel. I think city boys have no respect for animals."

"We want to bury it in the back, Momma," Rosette said. "Leave your notebook and come on, Lacey."

"Rosette, don't let your cat see what you are doing. Feed him first," said Mrs. DiNalli, "then bury the bird. That cat won't be so nosey if he's got a full stomach."

While Mrs. DiNalli was talking to Rosette, Lacey put her notebook on the green couch. Looking around, she noticed that the living room rug was a matching green and so was the overstuffed chair by the fireplace. On the mantel over the fireplace was a statue of a woman in a white gown with a blue shawl over her head and a red heart on the outside of her gown. Lacey recognized it as a statue of the Virgin Mary.

She liked the room. It made her feel more at home than their own living room, where the floor and walls were still bare and boxes still stood unpacked along the edges.

"Nice you came to visit, Lacey."

Lacey started, suddenly aware that Mrs. DiNalli had spoken to her. "Thank you," she said politely,

"I'm glad I came." She followed Rosette through the dining room into the kitchen.

Rosette got out an old newspaper, laid it on a kitchen chair and set the dead pigeon on it. Then she went to a cupboard.

Lacey stood at the back door, looking at the backyards of the other double houses. On her left the view was blocked by a brick building jutting out. Lacey remembered the empty store and decided that was what the building was. A high chain-link fence enclosed all the land behind the house. Lacey stared at it, wondering why it looked so familiar.

"Come on," Rosette said, carrying a bowl of some kind of smelly meat, "I want to show you something."

Lacey reached for the pigeon but Rosette shook her head. "Not now," she said, stepping onto the back porch. Lacey followed. They went down the back steps into a dirt yard. There was no grass, only a scattering of weeds.

"I tried to grow a garden once," Rosette said, "but no luck. My dad says the soil is probably worn out."

Lacey had a strange feeling she had been there before, in that dirt yard, yet she knew that was not possible.

Rosette set the bowl down near the back porch steps, then called loudly, "Here, kitty, kitty, kitty!"

Lacey heard a loud miaow and looked up; peering

down from the roof of the store building was the yellow cat!

"You!" she said. She turned to Rosette. "Is that *your* cat?"

Rosette laughed. "Sure. Why not? Just because I don't have a pony doesn't mean I can't have any pets. How come you look so funny?"

Lacey wasn't sure she could answer that. Somehow it had never occurred to her that the cat across the way would really belong to someone, especially to someone she knew.

She ran to the end of the brick building. There was the old ladder. Turning to the chain-link fence nearby, she could see the parking lot and the apartment building beyond it. She searched the third floor for a certain window with pink curtains and a balcony. There it was — her own window. There was no doubt about it. Rosett's cat was the yellow cat.

Lacey hurried back to Rosette. The yellow cat had come down the ladder and was eating the food in the bowl. Lacey bent to pet him, but suddenly stopped herself. She was afraid that if she touched him, the special bond she had felt would be broken and he would turn out to be just another cat. So she contented herself with just watching him.

It was the first time she had seen him up close, and she noticed things she hadn't seen from far off. Like the fluffy golden ruff at his throat which made him look very proud, and the stiff white whiskers that jutted out on either side of his face, with sparse white eyebrows to match.

"He's a beautiful cat, Rosette," Lacey said admiringly.

"You started to pet him before — go on, don't be afraid. He's tame."

Lacey had to smile at hearing him called tame. "He's goofy," she said. Unable to resist the look of his soft yellow fur any longer, she bent down and gently petted him.

"He sure is! But how do you know that? You've never seen him before, have you?"

"Maybe I have and maybe I haven't," Lacey said, trying to sound very mysterious.

"What do you mean by that?"

Lacey giggled at the strange look on Rosette's face. Then, motioning for Rosette to follow her, she walked over to the fence on the store side of the yard and pointed to her own apartment building beyond the parking lot. "See that window with the pink curtains? On the third floor, by the balcony?"

When Rosette had found it, Lacey said, "That's *my* window. That's where we live. I can see your yard and the store building and the second floor of your house from there. I've been watching your yellow cat ever since I moved in last Thursday. I didn't know whose cat he was, I just liked watching him."

"You know," Rosette said thoughtfully, "we really don't live very far from each other at all. If this fence weren't here, you could cut across the parking lot and be home in less than a minute."

"That's right," Lacey agreed.

"Or if you were a monkey," Rosette went on, giggling, "you could climb over the fence — except it's ten feet tall, my dad says. And that barbed wire at the top is there to keep people from trying to climb over."

At the mention of the barbed wire, Lacey told Rosette about the cat's attempt to climb the fence.

"I've never seen him do that," Rosette said. "I always thought he was happy out here. Maybe he's not. Maybe he's lonely."

"Can't you have him in the house with you?"

"No. He used to stay inside when he was a kitten," Rosette explained as they walked back to the cat who was rapidly devouring the cat food in his bowl. "But when he got older, he started to sharpen his claws on the furniture. He practically ruined the sides of that green chair in the living room. So Momma made me put him outside."

"That's too bad," Lacey said sympathetically. "What does he do in the winter?"

"Well, on very cold nights, he sleeps in the basement. But usually he sleeps in a wooden box under the porch."

They both knelt to pet the yellow cat. When Lacey felt the soft warmth of his body again, she was glad she had let herself touch him. He wasn't a special set-apart thing any longer, that was true. But now he was alive to her in a new way.

"Hey! He's wearing a collar!" she exclaimed when her fingers brushed against firm leather at his neck.

"What's wrong with that?" Rosette said. "Dogs wear collars, so I figured my cat could, too. I know of an old lady who not only has a collar on her cat, but puts a leash on him and takes him for a walk every day."

Lacey choked back a giggle. She didn't want to give the impression that she was laughing at Rosette. "You don't do *that*, do you?" she asked carefully.

Rosette snickered. "No! I wouldn't do anything that goofy. But with a collar on him, I figured if he ever got lost, people would know whose cat he was. See? There's a tag on the collar."

Lacey bent to read the metal tag: "My name is Beauregard. I belong to Rosette DiNalli, 16642 Lascana Street, Cleveland, Ohio."

Beauregard! The name didn't seem to fit him. For Lacey he had become "the yellow cat" and would always be that. But she didn't say anything to Rosette. Instead she smoothed her hand over the cat's back and felt it arch against her.

"Having a collar makes sense, Rosette," she said.

They watched the yellow cat as he sat down, licked his paw and cleaned his face with it.

"I love animals, don't you?" Lacey said, suddenly wanting to share with Rosette.

"Yes. Better than people sometimes. Know what I mean?"

Lacey nodded. "Sometimes people don't seem to care about you. But an animal always loves you."

"That's right," Rosette said firmly. "I knew you'd understand, Lacey."

Together they sat watching the cat until he darted away to stalk a pigeon that had landed in the yard. Then together they went to find a burial place for the other pigeon in the kitchen.

8

T<small>HEY</small> chose a place in the shadow of the store building, where it would be cool in summer and protected from the wind in winter. Rosette had found a piece of soft green flannel that had once been one of her nightgowns. They wrapped it carefully around the dead pigeon. Then, with Mr. DiNalli's shovel, they dug a hole and lowered the cloth-wrapped bird into it. Gently they filled the hole with dirt again. On the top they put small flat stones as grave markers.

"That looks very nice," Rosette said, smoothing away the extra stones and loose dirt.

"Yes, it does," Lacey agreed. "You know, you could make this into a cemetery. You could put a little fence around it and have it as a special place to bury city animals that die."

"That's a good idea, Lacey. But wouldn't the cat bother it?"

"I don't think so. A dog might dig up buried things, but not a cat. They don't like dirt on their food."

"How do you know that?"

"I had a cemetery at home, behind our garage. It was a bird-rabbit-chipmunk cemetery. I covered the ground around it with moss and planted a flower at the head of each grave. And no cats ever bothered it."

"You did? Well, we don't have moss, but maybe Momma would let us have some of her plants," Rosette said eagerly. Then she frowned. "No, that won't work."

"Why not?"

"Nothing'll grow in this dumb soil!" Rosette plopped herself onto the ground.

"Well, why couldn't we use plastic flowers?" Lacey said quickly, the idea just coming to her. "They aren't as nice as real ones, but at least they'd still be blooming in the middle of winter when real ones are gone."

Rosette grinned. "You know, you have more good

ideas than anybody in the world . . . except me, of course!"

"Thanks, Rosette." Lacey spoke offhandedly but she was pleased. "Some people don't like a person who has lots of ideas."

"Some people are just dopes," Rosette said, tossing her head and making her long dark hair fly about wildly.

Lacey ran her fingers wistfully through her own short hair. "You have pretty hair, Rosette," she said. "Want to hear what I think it looks like?"

"I know." Rosette made a face. "A mop. That's what my daddy says."

"Oh, no!" Lacey said, astonished that anyone would think that. "It looks like a horse's mane!"

Lacey waited to see if Rosette would laugh or get mad. But she didn't do either. She smiled — not a funny-face smile, but a real one.

"You're the only one who's ever noticed," she said. "I've never told anyone because I knew they'd laugh, but that's what I think it looks like, too. Sort of like an Arabian stallion's, don't you think?"

"It does, Rosette, it does! I have a book called *King of the Wind*. It's about Arabian horses, and in it there's a picture of two stallions fighting. Their manes are flying and they're beautiful. Your hair looks just like that."

Rosette pulled at a dark strand. "It really does,

huh? That's great. Hey!" She got to her feet and stuck out a hand to Lacey. "Where is your picture of your pony?"

"In my notebook in the living room," Lacey said, letting Rosette help pull her up.

"Come on, I want to show it to my mother."

Hand-in-hand they ran up the porch steps and burst into the DiNalli kitchen.

"Momma, Lacey had a pony," Rosette told her mother. "She's got a picture of him. Show Momma, Lacey."

Lacey went into the living room to get the picture. Seeing a telephone on a table reminded her that she hadn't called her mother. She took the picture of Tiny Joe into the kitchen to Mrs. DiNalli and asked to use the phone.

After she had called home she went back to the kitchen, where Mrs. DiNalli and Rosette were studying the picture.

"He looks like a nice pony," Mrs. DiNalli said. "You had to sell him?"

"Yes, Momma. But she sold him to a good friend."

Lacey stiffened. She hoped Rosette wouldn't talk about Pam. "He is a nice pony," she said quickly, "but my dad called him a troublemaker. One summer, before we built him the stall in the garage, we boarded him in a farmer's pasture. There were cows in the pasture too."

Lacey talked fast, not giving either Rosette or Mrs. DiNalli a chance to break in.

"And one week the farmer's cows got out every day. Every time the farmer went to get the cows to milk them, the gate to the pasture would be open and the cows scattered all over. Well, they finally found out that it was Tiny Joe who was opening the gate. So the farmer wouldn't let us keep him in the pasture any more. That's when Daddy helped me build a stall in the garage for him."

Rosette and Mrs. DiNalli laughed at Lacey's story. Then Mrs. DiNalli handed the picture back to Lacey and said, "Rosette, why don't you take Lacey upstairs to your room and show her your horse collection?"

Lacey breathed a soft sigh of relief as she followed Rosette out of the kitchen.

Rosette took the stairs two at a time and Lacey did the same. They passed one room where the door was closed. "That's my grandmother's room," Rosette explained; "she lives with us."

"Don't you have any brothers or sisters either?" Lacey asked.

Rosette shook her head.

Lacey looked thoughtful. "That makes one more way we're alike," she said.

Rosette led the way into the end room that was painted a bright yellow. "This is my room," she announced.

The first thing Lacey saw was a bookshelf filled with horses. There were all sizes and shapes, from a large copper saddle horse to a small gray donkey with flowers through his teeth.

"You can pick them up if you want to," Rosette said. "I know you'll be careful."

Lacey put the picture on the bed and went to the bookcase. One by one she picked up each horse and held it lovingly in her hands. She forgot about the pigeon and the cat and even Rosette. She was back in Three Corners and each one was Tiny Joe, only different.

Something touched her arm, causing her to look around. Held out for her to see was a small blue box. And nestled in the box was a delicate, exquisitely carved ivory colt. It was so lifelike that it even had tiny baby whiskers on its muzzle.

"Oh, Pam," she said softly, "it's beautiful."

A loud snicker jarred her.

"What did you call me?" Rosette said.

Lacey frowned. "What do you mean?"

"You just called me Pam."

"No, I didn't. I couldn't have."

"Well, you did."

Lacey shook her head. She couldn't have done that, could she? She put the ivory colt back in its box, the spell of its charm broken.

"Well, you did," Rosette said again. "So what?

Everybody mixes up names sometimes. I'm sorry I laughed. Don't be mad. Come on, there are more horses to look at. See this one? An Indian carved him."

Lacey looked at the horse collection again, but the joy of seeing it had left her. She sat on Rosette's bed not really listening as Rosette continued to talk about each horse.

"What's the matter?" Rosette said after a few minutes. She stopped talking and sat down beside Lacey. "Don't you feel good?"

Lacey shrugged. "I feel okay." She reached for the picture of Tiny Joe.

"You really miss that pony, don't you?" Rosette said quietly.

Lacey ran her fingers along the pony's neck as if she were petting him. "More than anything, Rosette," she said. "And Pam and Three Corners, too. I guess that's why I called you Pam. I always think about her."

"I bet it's awful to move. I never have, and I never want to."

"It *is* awful," Lacey said, and suddenly she was telling Rosette all about it. How she had been forced to lead Tiny Joe into Pam's barn because he wouldn't go in without her. How he had nickered when she left him, as though he had known she was never coming back. And how she had found a handful of leftover oats in his feedbox when she got back from Pam's and it had made her cry so hard she couldn't stop.

Rosette's eyes filled with tears as she listened. "That *is* awful," she said. "Now your friend Pam has him. Is she taking good care of him?"

"I don't know, Rosette. That's just the trouble. She's my best friend but she hasn't even written to me about him."

"Well, she doesn't sound like much of a friend to me. She knows how much you love that pony. She should be more thoughtful."

"That's what I think." Lacey felt anger rising in her. "She could have at least written about him instead of all that dumb stuff about her 4-H sewing prize at the — " Lacey stopped abruptly, stunned by what she had just heard herself say.

Why had she said that? She hadn't meant to; the words had just slipped out. But why had . . . Rosette! Rosette had made her do it, had tricked her into saying something nasty about Pam. Lacey turned and glared at Rosette. "That wasn't very nice of you," she said accusingly.

"What wasn't?"

"You made me talk against my best friend. Just when I was beginning to think you were a friend."

Rosette got off the bed. "You're nuts," she said. "I didn't make you do anything. You did it yourself. You said that about your friend because that's the way you feel. And if you ask me, you're right. She sounds like a dope to me."

Rosette snatched the picture off Lacey's lap. "Who cares about sewing when you could have a pony like this?"

"She is too a friend. Don't say that! And you give me back my picture!" Lacey lunged and tried to grab the picture.

"No," said Rosette, laughing and ducking out of Lacey's reach. "He's mine, all mine," she chanted as she clasped the picture to her heart.

"*Give my my picture!*" Lacy demanded, suddenly feeling very cold.

"Oh, Lacey, don't get mad. I was only teasing," Rosette said. "You're the touchiest person in the whole world."

"I wouldn't talk if I were you," Lacey snapped, stung by Rosette's accusation. "You're the bossiest. And you exaggerate, and that's worse."

"I do not. Just for that, I'll never give you back your picture."

"Oh, yes, you will," Lacey said, scrambling over the bed. "Right now!"

She forced Rosette into a corner, gripped her arm with one hand and with the other tugged at the picture. Suddenly there was a small sound and the picture was in her hand. She had won!

Then she looked at it, and gasped. She only had half of the picture. "You tore my picture," she cried, "my only picture!"

Rosette handed her the other half. "I'm sorry, Lacey," she said. "I didn't mean for it to tear. I was only teasing you."

"You tore it on purpose!" Lacey said angrily. "I know you did. You're a mean person and I'm never coming to your house again!"

Lacey dashed out of the bedroom and down the stairs. She didn't even stop to speak to Mrs. DiNalli. She just grabbed up her notebook from the living room and ran out the front door.

9

When Lacey got home, she wouldn't tell her mother what was wrong. She went straight to her room and shut the door. Matching the torn edges as well as she could, she Scotch-taped the two pieces of Tiny Joe's picture together. It was in one piece again, but she knew it would never be the same. Rosette was to blame for that — mean, stupid Rosette who got to live in a house and have an animal of her own to take care of.

Lacey lay on her bed and made faces at the tiny cracks in the ceiling plaster, hating even them because they were a part of this new life, too.

A loud miaow drew her out of her thoughts. She got off the bed and went to the window. The yellow cat was on the roof, jumping over imaginary hurdles. Lacey felt a little stab of regret. Now that she knew whose cat he was, she would never again enjoy watching him. She jerked down the window blind and went back to the bed.

After a few minutes, Lacey heard her father come home from work. She wanted desperately to run to him, hug him, and tell him what had happened. But she couldn't. She just lay in the dimly lit room, listening to the sounds of her mother getting supper.

A little while later there was a knock on her door. "Supper's ready, dear," her mother called softly. "Do you feel like eating?"

Reluctantly Lacey got up off the bed and went into the bathroom to wash her hands. She wasn't hungry, but she was tired of being alone.

At the table no one asked her any questions. They just let her eat in silence. For that she was glad. It was only as they were finishing dessert that her mother asked, "Lacey, is that paint on the front of your dress?"

Lacey looked down. She hadn't noticed it before, but there was something — a spot of blood where she had held the pigeon close to protect it from Willie Thompson. She looked up to tell what it was and to her surprise burst into tears.

Her father pulled her into his lap. "Tell us what's wrong, Lace," he said, gently wiping the tears from her cheeks.

But Lacey sat stiff and silent in her father's lap.

"Please tell us, dear," said her mother. "We know you're unhappy about something."

"I'm unhappy because I don't like it here!" Lacey finally blurted out. "And I don't like Rosette. She laughed at me and tore my picture of Tiny Joe."

Lacey felt her father's arms tighten around her. "How did that happen, Lace?"

Lacey tried to jump off her father's lap, but he held her fast. "Why did she laugh at you?" he asked.

"Because . . . because I called her Pam," Lacey said, wishing they wouldn't ask her any more questions.

"And you had a fight because she laughed at you? That doesn't sound like you, Lace."

Lacey looked up at her father. "Please, Daddy, let me go. Please?"

"All right, Lace. But first I want you to listen to me. I don't know what caused all this, but I have an idea. You've been unhappy here because you've had to leave all your friends behind, isn't that right?"

Lacey nodded.

"And then along comes a new friend and you think you're being disloyal to your old friend if you like her too. Right?"

Lacey shook her head hard. "No. I don't like Rosette. She's not my friend; Pam is."

"Listen, Lace," her father went on, "you mustn't be upset if you find yourself liking new people. That's the way life is. It doesn't mean you love your old friends less; it just means you love them in a different way. Don't you see?"

"No, I don't," Lacey said firmly. Her father wasn't making sense.

Then her mother spoke. "When I was a little girl, Lacey, I had a best friend just like you do. One day she moved to New Jersey. I missed her so much, I thought I would never get over it. And I was sure I'd never see her again. But you know what? We still write to each other. After all these years, we're still friends. We're not as close as we were then, but we're still friends."

Lacey frowned. All those words. Her parents kept saying a lot of words, but what they were really telling her to do was to forget Pam and forget Tiny Joe. She couldn't do that. She was a friend who remembered, not a friend who forgot.

"No, no!" she cried. "I don't want new friends, I want Pam and Tiny Joe. I love them. I'll always love them. I don't *want* to forget them!"

With that, she tried again to jump from her father's lap, and this time he let her go. She ran to her room, slamming the door behind her, unable to make sense out of anything.

It didn't seem like Friday to her when she started to school the next day. It seemed more like Monday, her first day — a day when she had gone to an unfamiliar place with unfamiliar faces and had felt completely alone.

It wasn't her first day, though. She knew which line to get into now, and she knew some faces . . . one in particular which she would avoid.

Lacey walked into the room and took her seat. She had spoken to no one in line. She spoke to no one in the room. And no one spoke to her. Mrs. Klein was busy at the blackboard, and Betsy, who sometimes spoke, was away from her seat. Rosette wasn't in the room yet.

As she settled her things Lacey heard Willie Thompson say something about "the bird girl." She ignored him. But when Willie shouted, "There's the other bird girl!" she knew that Rosette was coming.

Lacey pretended to be very busy at her desk. She wasn't going to speak to Rosette or even act as if she knew she had come in.

"Hi, Lacey," she heard Rosette say, "still mad at me?"

Lacey didn't answer. Not then or any other time that morning did she even look in Rosette's direction.

On the playground after lunch, Rosette spoke to her again. "Lacey, I'm sorry," she said. "I know that picture meant a lot to you."

Lacey turned away.

"Okay," snapped Rosette. "If you're going to be like that, so am I. Who cares about your silly old picture anyway?" With that, she walked off.

Lacey gave Rosette's back a cold stare. She didn't think Rosette was really sorry. And how could she ever have thought Rosette's hair was pretty? It wasn't at all; it was long and stringy. Rosette was fat, too. And probably couldn't ride very well. Horse-lovers stick together! Not if Rosette was one of them.

Right after that, in class, she saw Rosette pass a note to Betsy. Betsy nodded, looked at Lacey, and giggled.

Then Lacey heard Rosette whisper just loud enough for her to hear: "And if she doesn't like it here, why doesn't she go back where she came from?"

Lacey's stomach churned. So that was the way Rosette felt about her. Well, she was glad to know. It made it all the easier to ignore her.

Rosette didn't try to be friendly any more. Lacey was glad. When the three o'clock bell rang, she gathered up her things and rushed toward the door.

"Have a terrible weekend," she heard Rosette shout after her.

She turned abruptly and for the first time that day spoke to Rosette: "The same to you. The very same to you!" she said and ran from the room.

She beat the boys out of school, so there was no one at the candy store to bother her. As she hurried past it she tried not to think about what had taken place there yesterday. Yet she could still hear Rosette shouting, "Cut it out, Thompson. You leave her alone!" Rosette had stood up against the biggest boy in the class to help her.

But that was before, and this was after. And besides, it was too late. Lacey ran upstairs, eager to get her mind on something else besides Rosette.

That was impossible, though, as long as she kept the window blind down. The drawn blind was a constant reminder. Lacey kept imagining the scene behind it: Rosette's cat chasing paper in the yard . . . a freshly dug grave . . .

She braced herself as she began to feel a strong urge to lift the blind and peek at the yellow cat.

To make certain she would not be tempted again, she went into the living room to read until supper time. And that night she went to bed with the blind still down.

10

THE NEXT MORNING Lacey woke early, as she always did on weekends. But because her room was so dark, she thought it was still night. Then she saw the edging of light around the drawn blind and knew it must be morning.

She got out of bed and lifted the shade to peek out. It was morning, but the cat was not in sight. Ashamed of herself for being so weak, she slapped the blind down and went back to bed.

Saturdays in Three Corners had always been something to look forward to. In the mornings she used to help her mother in the house. Then, on the afternoons that her father had off from his route, they would be outside together, digging in the garden, exercising the pony; or in winter, shoveling snow off the walk and the driveway.

There would be none of that now. There was no garden, no pony, and no walk. Lacey sighed and tried to go back to sleep, but it was no use. She was wide awake and dying to watch the yellow cat.

She buried her head under her pillow to keep from seeing the window blind. As she did, she heard a knock on the door. Pulling her head out, she asked, "Who's there?"

The door opened. There was her father standing in the doorway, his face covered with shaving lather. "I came to kiss you good morning," he said, grinning.

"Oh, Daddy, go away, please." Lacey didn't feel like being joked with.

Her father came toward her. "What? Go away without getting a kiss from my own daughter? Impossible!"

With a loud yelp Lacey buried her head under the pillow again, feeling the bed sag as her father sat down on it and began to tickle her. She held her breath for as long as she could but gave in at last and burst out laughing.

Immediately the pillow was lifted off her head. "See? It doesn't hurt to laugh once in a while, does it?" her father said, smiling. "Now get out of that bed. We're going somewhere.

Lacey sprang up. "Where?"

"I have this Saturday off, and I'm taking you and Mother for a drive around Cleveland."

"Oh." Lacey flopped back. "I don't want to go."

"You don't, huh?" said her father, pinning her arms to the bed and leaning over her. "Maybe instead you'd like a nice lathery kiss?"

"No, no, Daddy," Lacey shouted and turned her head just as his face came down. She felt the shaving cream on her cheek and smelled its fragrance as her father kissed her. Then she hugged him, saying: "Okay, you win. I'll go, too."

After breakfast, Lacey, her mother, and her father went down to the parking lot. Lacey saw the yellow cat in the yard standing on his hind legs, swatting at flies with his forepaws. She quickly got in the car and shut her eyes, keeping them shut until the car was out of the parking lot and headed toward the light at Woodhill. After that she opened them and looked out the window.

"There's the Woodhill Road Rapid Transit stop," said her father as they were driving along. "Someday we'll all take that downtown to the Terminal Tower Building. Would you like that, Lace?"

"Yes, Daddy, that would be nice," Lacey said, but she didn't really care if she ever saw the Terminal Tower Building, whatever that was. She knew now why they were taking a ride — to convince her to like Cleveland. It was hard to like Cleveland, though, when there was another place she liked better.

They passed houses, stores, gas stations, and apartment buildings. After driving down a long hill where there were many trees and a deep ravine, they came to a place where all the roads seemed to cross each other. There Lacey saw a long placid lake surrounded by grassy banks. At the far end of the lake was a large gray columned building.

"Is that the Mayor's house?" she asked.

Her mother and father laughed. "That's the Cleveland Art Museum," her father said. "Want to park the car and walk around the lake? I think there are some swans there."

"No, thank you," Lacey said.

"Let's drive around it then, Stan," said her mother.

Lacey tried not to look, but she spotted a squirrel on the grass and was caught up by his efforts to beg food from the people seated on the white benches that lined the walkways around the lagoon.

"You could come down here for Saturday morning art lessons sometime if you wanted to, Lacey," said her father as he drove the car slowly around the museum. "Or you could go to the Natural Science Museum, or just stand there and smell the roses." He pointed to an enormous bed of roses.

Lacey read the sign: ROSE GARDENS. She shook her head.

"No sale, eh?" he said. "Well, there's another place I was told about that will be sure to interest you. It's out east a way. Here we go!"

Lacey looked through the back window as they drove away from the Art Museum. She searched for the swans but never saw them.

Soon they were on Lakeshore Drive where cars rushed by steadily. On her left was a very large body of water that never seemed to end. She wondered what it was.

"That's Lake Erie," said her father, as though he had read her mind. "One of the five Great Lakes. Know how it was formed? By a glacier."

Lacey stared at the water. Far out, there was a big black boat, and way beyond it the sky came down and met the lake. "Is Canada over there somewhere?" she asked finally.

"That's right, Lace. How'd you know that?"

"We studied about Canada last spring in Three Corners."

"Oh," said her father.

After that, there was no more talk. They drove for

such a long, long time that Lacey grew tired of sitting. "When will we get there?" she asked.

"Soon," came the reply as they left the big highway for a smaller two-laned street.

The windows of the car were open and over the noise of the rushing wind Lacey began to hear people screaming and circus music playing. She leaned forward to see what was happening.

They were just passing a strange-looking wooden structure that was all high hills, dips, and curves when suddenly the screams grew louder and a little open train-like thing full of people went zooming past on the wooden structure.

Lacey watched it chug up a hill, then disappear over the other side as the screams echoed loudly again. "That looks like a roller coaster," she said excitedly. "Is it a fair, Daddy?"

"No, it's not a fair, Lace. It's Euclid Beach Amusement Park. Want to go in?"

"Yes, let's go!" Lacey bounced on the seat, turning her head this way and that in order to see everything.

They parked the car and walked toward the amusement section. They rode on everything: the roller coaster, the dodge-'em, the high-flying, silver-bodied zeppelins that seemed to sweep over the lake as they slowly circled their base poles.

They went into the fun house, and through a dark, mysterious tunnel where things leaped out and made Lacey scream. They ate hot dogs and more hot dogs and ice cream and root beer and popcorn. They even watched some Scottish kilt dancers do a sword dance to the wailing sounds of bagpipes.

By late afternoon they were all tired and ready to go. Lacey climbed in the front seat between her mother and father, and rested her head on her mother's shoulder as they drove.

"Did you have fun, Lace?" asked her father a little while later.

Lacey remembered the look of fright on her mother's face as they swooped down a steep hill on the roller coaster, and giggled. "Yes, it *was* lots of fun, Daddy."

"Maybe sometime we could come again and bring your friend, Rosette," her mother suggested.

Lacey sobered instantly. Why did Rosette have to be mentioned? Somehow it made the whole day seem like a trick.

Lifting her head from her mother's shoulder, she sat up stiff and straight the rest of the way home.

11

Lacey woke early Sunday morning, too. She tiptoed into the kitchen to see what time it was and peered at the clock through sleep-puffy eyes. Six o'clock! There was a faint cough from the living room. Lacey looked in. Her father, sitting up in bed reading, silently waved to her and she waved back. She saw that her mother was still asleep.

Lacey sighed and went back to her room. What

was there to do this early? She was going to church with her mother and father at eleven, but that was five hours from now.

She flung herself onto the bed. The blind was still down, and for a long time she stared at it, thinking that maybe she should let herself have just one look. That wouldn't be the same as sitting for hours and admiring Rosette's cat.

Finally Lacey got up, walked to the window, and lifted the edge of the blind. Yes, there he was, at the far side of the DiNalli lot. But what was he doing? Oh, no! He wasn't going to try to climb that fence again! Lacey groaned inwardly. That was just what he was going to do — the dumb cat!

Lacey let go of the blind in disgust. Why should she care what the silly cat was doing? He was Rosette's lookout, not hers. She went to her closet and pulled on a pair of blue jeans, a blouse, and her sneakers. She might as well get dressed. There was nothing else to do at six o'clock in the morning.

But after dressing, she found herself drawn to the window again. She peeked out. The cat was still climbing. He had reached the first strand of barbed wire and was stretching carefully for the next. Lacey stood transfixed. Now he had all four paws on the two lower strands and was trying to keep his balance as he reached for the highest one.

Without warning he began to wobble dizzily. Suddenly his hind legs slipped off the wire. Lacey cried out, expecting to see him go plunging to the ground. But he didn't; he hung there with his head and front paws caught in the twisted strands of wire.

"His collar," Lacey whispered, "his collar is caught."

She watched him give a mighty kick to free himself.

"Oh, don't, cat, don't. You'll choke yourself. Oh, why don't you scream or yowl to wake up Rosette?"

Rosette! Lacey frowned. Her thoughts were coming too fast and she felt confused. Why was she so worried about that girl's cat anyway? She tried to turn away from the window, to ignore the struggle going on, but she couldn't. She wouldn't. She loved that cat and she knew Rosette did too. She had to try to save him.

Lacey ran from her room. She saw the startled look on her father's face as she burst through the hall into the living room. "Rosette's cat is in trouble," she whispered hoarsely as she opened the door. "I'm going to help it."

Without waiting for her father to reply, she raced out of the apartment, the door banging loudly after her.

Down the three flights of stairs and out the back door to the parking lot she ran. Across the lot and to the chain-link fence. On the other side of the DiNalli

lot she saw the cat. He was still hanging, still struggling.

"Rosette! Rosette!" she yelled, her voice echoing in the early stillness. "Wake up! Your cat is in trouble!"

Not waiting for an answer, Lacey stretched her arms over her head the way she had seen the cat stretch up his paws. She found fingerholds in the diamond-shaped mesh of the fence, then toe holds. She pulled herself upward, straining for speed as her fingers felt the painful pressure of the round wire.

She glanced at the cat again. He was still moving. She looked toward the house. In an upper story window an old woman with gray hair stood watching her.

"Wake Rosette!" she yelled. "Wake Rosette. Her cat's choking!"

The old woman didn't seem to understand her, and Lacey couldn't let go to point at the cat. So she kept yelling, "The cat! the cat!" as she inched her way up the fence.

"Oh, if I only had that ladder," she whispered through gritted teeth, seeing the ladder propped against the end of the store building.

Just as she reached the top of the chain-link and stretched for a hold on the barbed wire overhead, she heard a terrible yowl. Looking across the yard, she saw the cat give one great convulsive kick, free itself from the barbed-wire strangle hold, and plummet to the ground.

"Oh, no!" she cried. "Help . . . help!" she shouted. "Daddy! Rosette! Come quickly! Oh, why doesn't somebody hear me?"

Just then a big man in pajamas came dashing into the yard. And behind him came Rosette, looking scared. They rushed to the fallen cat.

"Rosette, Rosette!" Lacey shouted, "is he all right?"

Rosette glanced up in Lacey's direction and waved, then hurriedly turned her attention back to the cat.

"Lacey, are *you* all right?" a voice suddenly called from behind.

Lacey looked around. Running toward the fence, buttoning their clothes as they came, were her mother and father.

"Oh, Daddy," Lacey cried. "I'm all right, but the cat's been badly hurt."

"Where is the cat, Lace?" Her father was now standing directly below her.

Forgetting where she was in her concern for the cat, Lacey pointed across the lot. At that same moment, she lost her toe hold in the wire. She felt herself falling and grabbed with her pointing hand. She cried out in pain as a barb bit into her palm. But she managed to cling there, with one hand on the round top of the chain-link fence, one clamped around the barbed wire, and her feet struggling for another hold.

"Let go," commanded her father, "I'll catch you."

Lacey was startled to find herself too weak to hang on. Her hands let go and she felt herself drop. "I'm falling, Daddy!" she screamed.

She landed safely in her father's arms. Her mother kissed her and tried to tend to her hand, but Lacey jerked it free. "No, it's all right. What about the cat? Where is it?"

They looked across the yard, but Rosette and her father had disappeared. "Come on," Lacey said. "They live on the other side of this store building."

Lacey ran ahead, with her mother and father following. As she pounded up the porch steps of Rosette's house, the old woman with the gray hair opened the door for them.

"Where is the cat?" Lacey asked breathlessly.

The woman pointed to the kitchen. All three hurried through the house to where they could see Rosette and her mother and father gathered around the kitchen table.

Rosette's father was squeezing the cat's chest when they came in. Rosette turned to Lacey and whimpered, "Oh, Lacey, he hasn't moved since we picked him up. Daddy's trying to help him breathe. That awful collar choked him, didn't it?"

Lacey stared at the yellow body, rusty in spots from blood. She nodded as she put out a hand to comfort Rosette.

"Maybe . . . maybe we'll have something else to bury in our cemetery," Rosette said, starting to cry.

"Now, take it easy, Rose," said Mr. DiNalli. "Crying won't help him."

"Shouldn't we take him to an animal doctor?" asked Lacey's father.

Mr. DiNalli nodded thoughtfully. "Yes, I think we'd better. I can't seem to bring him around. There's an animal clinic on 131st Street off Union. Rosette, you and Momma call and tell them we're coming as soon as we can get there with an unconscious bleeding cat. Then you get dressed."

Rosette and Mrs. DiNalli hurried out of the kitchen. Lacey and her mother and father moved closer and asked if there was anything they could do to help.

"I'm Barto DiNalli," Rosette's father said. "Do you have a car, Mr. Lewis? Mine is in the garage being repaired."

Lacey's father nodded. "I'll bring it right around," he said.

"Lacey," Mr. DiNalli said, stepping aside, "can you hold the sides of this cut together? We mustn't let it dry out before we get the cat to the doctor. I've got to get dressed too."

Lacey reached out to gently push together the two edges of torn flesh. As she did, blood oozed out, and she had to bite her lips to keep from gagging.

Soon Rosette came rushing back. "We got the clinic. They'll be ready for us when we get there. How is he, Lacey?"

Lacey kept her eyes on the yellow cat so she wouldn't betray to Rosette her deep worry. "I don't know," she said softly. "I just don't know."

12

WHEN Rosette's father came back to the kitchen a few minutes later, Lacey was surprised to see him in a policeman's uniform. That explained how he knew so much about emergency treatment of animals, though. And it explained something else: why the boys had run from the candy store the other day when Rosette threatened to tell her father. They all had known he was a policeman.

"Okay, girls," he said, "Lacey's father is outside with the car. You *are* coming with us, aren't you, Lacey?"

Lacey looked quickly at her mother who nodded and said, "Go ahead. I'll stay here and keep Mrs. DiNalli company."

"I'll take him now, Lacey." Mr. DiNalli gently slid one hand under the cat's body while he held the cut together with the other. "You girls go ahead of me and get the doors open," he said.

Lacey and Rosette did as they were told. When they were all in the car, Mr. DiNalli said, "Turn right onto Woodhill, Mr. Lewis. Union is south, past the school."

Lacey's father put the car into gear and soon they were speeding along Woodhill. They passed the school, then a gas station where Lacey got a glimpse of a clock. It was thirteen minutes after six! All of this had happened in just thirteen minutes, but to Lacey it had seemed like hours.

While she was looking out the window for Union, her hand began to sting. Without thinking she rubbed it, then cried out in pain. It was the hand that had gotten torn on the barbed wire.

"Oh, Lacey!" Rosette said. "How did you do that?"

"On the barbed wire," Lacey said. "When I started to fall I grabbed it."

"We'll have the doctor fix that, too," Mr. DiNalli said. "Turn left at the third stop light, Mr. Lewis. That's Union. Go down it to 131st Street and turn right. The clinic is on the left-hand side, a small yellow-brick building set back from the road. Watch for it, girls."

As soon as they were on 131st Street, Rosette and Lacey began to watch closely. "There it is, there it is," they shouted, spotting it at the same time.

Lacey's father turned into the circular gravel drive, parked the car in front of the building, and got out to open the door for Mr. DiNalli. Silently the girls followed.

The veterinarian was inside waiting for them. From some other part of the hospital, dogs barked, but the doctor ignored them. "In here, Officer," he said and led the way into a room where there were cabinets full of bottles and instruments and where a gray metal stretcher stood in the middle of the floor. A strong smell of medicine was all about the room.

The veterinarian looked at the girls. "Don't you two want to sit in the waiting room?"

Lacey looked at Rosette. "We want to stay," they said. "Please let us."

"All right," said the doctor. "But if you start feeling faint, go outside and sit down."

Rosette's father put the cat on the stretcher table

and the veterinarian went to work. Quickly he cleaned out the cut with antiseptic.

Lacey tried to breathe through her mouth only so she wouldn't smell the medicine. But it was no use, the odor still penetrated. Rosette had stepped back almost to the door and was actually covering her nose.

The doctor spoke quietly to the two fathers. "While he is still comatose, I'm going to suture the cut. Then I'll administer oxygen. That should bring him around."

None of that made sense to Lacey until she saw the doctor take a needle with thick yellowish thread in it and begin to sew up the wound. All at once she felt dizzy. She began to stumble backward.

"Lacey, go outside!" she heard her father say sharply.

Both girls rushed from the operating room, through the stark waiting room, to fresh air outside. They both breathed deeply.

"Wasn't that awful?" Rosette gasped.

Lacey nodded, still sucking in air.

"Poor Beauregard. Oh, Lacey, I hope he doesn't die!"

"Don't say that, Rosette. Don't. Come on, let's wait in the car. I feel kind of weak."

The girls sat waiting in the car for a long time. Then, at last, they saw their fathers coming out. Mr.

DiNalli was carrying the yellow cat, still stretched out in his arms. The doctor, a piece of white gauze in his hand, came with them.

"The doctor wants to look at your cut, Lacey," her father said.

Lacey held out her hand. The doctor examined it, then said, "I want to sterilize this, Lacey. Grit your teeth because it's going to sting."

Lacey clamped her jaws tight while Rosette moved close to her as if to help her share the pain. When the doctor swabbed the scratch, Lacey jumped.

"There," he said, "good girl! It's only a surface scratch. I don't think you'll need tetanus shots."

"Thanks, Doctor," said Mr. DiNalli as he eased the yellow cat onto Rosette's lap.

"Glad to help, Officer," the doctor said. Then he spoke to Rosette. "I think your cat will be all right, but you will need to keep him warm and comfortable. In a few hours, if he will take it, give him water in small amounts. Then maybe a little food. A small amount of baby food smeared on his mouth might do the trick. He'll be too weak to stand up and eat. Call me if you have any questions."

"Thank you, Doctor," Rosette said softly. She smoothed the rumpled fur body on her lap.

Lacey's father started the car and soon they were heading back.

A short time later, Rosette and Lacey were in Rosette's bedroom. The yellow cat was lying in a cardboard box which they had lined with the rest of Rosette's old green flannel nightgown.

"Thank you, Lacey, for saving my cat," Rosette said.

Lacey shook her head. "I didn't save him, Rosette, your father did. I couldn't even get over the fence."

"Well, if it hadn't been for you, we would never have known he was in trouble. When Nonna heard you yelling, she got Daddy out of bed. How did you know he was caught?"

"I woke up early and was looking out the window," Lacey said.

"It's a good thing that you and Nonna are early birds."

"At first . . ." Lacey started to speak, then hesitated.

"What?"

"At first, I wasn't going to help," Lacey admitted. "After what you said about me on Friday."

"What? What did I say, Lacey?"

"You know. About going back to Three Corners if I didn't like it here."

"Oh, yeah, I remember. Well, you were being snooty to me. And you always talked so much about

Three Corners and that Pam. I guess I just got mad. I didn't really mean what I said, though."

"You didn't?"

"No. You're the first friend I've ever had who likes animals as much as I do. You aren't going back to Three Corners, are you?"

Lacey reached into the box to stroke the yellow cat. "No," she said at last, "I guess not. I guess this is our home now."

"I'm glad," Rosette said, "then we can really be friends."

Just then Rosette's mother called to them from the foot of the stairs. Reluctantly they left the cat and went down to the living room. Rosette's father had gone to work. Lacey's mother and father were getting ready to go home.

"Couldn't *I* stay a while, please?" Lacey begged.

"No, Lacey," said her mother. "We have to have breakfast and get ready for church. And I know Rosette and her mother and grandmother have things to do before they go to church."

Rosette gasped. "Momma, do I have to go? I don't want to leave Beauregard. Please let me stay home today!"

"You know you can't miss Mass, Rosette," Mrs. DiNalli said gently.

"But there'll be nobody to stay with the cat."

"What time is your Mass, Rosette?" Lacey asked.

Rosette looked at her mother. "Which one are we going to, Momma?"

Mrs. DiNalli shrugged. "Why, Lacey?"

"Well, if you have an early one you can go to, *I* could stay with the cat. We don't go to our church until a quarter to eleven. I could stay until you get back, then I could go home and get ready. Couldn't I?" Lacey looked beseechingly at her mother and father.

Rosette spoke up quickly. "We could go to the eight o'clock mass, Momma. Nonna is dressed. And I'll hurry. Please?"

Lacey and Rosette saw Mrs. DiNalli exchange looks with Lacey's parents. Then all three smiled and the girls knew that Lacey's idea had been accepted.

"Thank you, Lacey," Rosette whispered. "You *do* have more good ideas than anybody I know."

Lacey smiled. "Except you, of course!"

"Of course!" Rosette giggled and ran upstairs to dress.

Lacey sat by the carton the whole time Rosette was gone. She watched the cat closely, hoping for some sign that he was reviving. Once she thought she saw an ear twitch, but it didn't move again so she couldn't be sure.

Then Rosette was back, and it was Lacey's turn to

hurry home and dress for church. "He didn't move," she said as she was leaving. "I hope he'll be okay."

"I'll watch him, Lacey. You're coming right back after church, aren't you?"

Lacey grinned. "A team of Percheron horses couldn't keep me away," she called as she ran from the bright yellow room and down the stairs.

When Lacey returned, Rosette had a small jar of baby food in one hand and an eye dropper in the other.

"What are those for?" Lacey asked.

"For the cat. Remember what the doctor said? About food and water? Well, this eye dropper is for water. And Momma went to the delicatessen a little while ago and bought some baby food. Come on."

Rosette filled the eye dropper with water from the bathroom faucet. She took it to the carton and squeezed a tiny bit into the cat's mouth. They both waited breathlessly for something to happen, but there was no movement at all.

"He's dying," Rosette cried.

"No! No!" Lacey said excitedly. "I think I saw the tip of his tail move. Try again."

Rosette squeezed another drop of water into the cat's mouth, but still nothing happened.

"Try the food," Lacey said. "Smear a tiny bit on

his mouth the way the doctor said. It's chicken. All cats like chicken."

Rosette dipped her finger into the jar. Then she touched the bit of baby-food chicken around the cat's mouth. As before with the water, nothing happened.

Then, while they stood waiting and watching, a tiny pink tongue appeared and licked the food.

13

THAT NIGHT, Lacey was so tired she could hardly keep her eyes open long enough to get into bed. She had stayed at Rosette's the whole afternoon and for supper that evening. They had eaten in Rosette's room so that they could be near the cat.

After he had so feebly licked that first bit of food, he had taken more and more, until finally he had opened his eyes and twitched his tail at them. When he did that, Rosette and Lacey had grabbed hands and whirled each other happily around the bedroom. He was going to live.

Now, as she snuggled into bed, Lacey looked at her scratched palm. It still hurt a little but she didn't mind. It was a small thing compared to what the cat had suffered.

Lacey turned out the light and shut her eyes. But just as everything was becoming smooth and soft and dim, she jerked suddenly awake. With a cry, she sat up and turned the light on again. She had forgotten to say good night to Tiny Joe!

How could that have happened? She had been up since early morning . . . that was it. She was just so tired that she had forgotten. Well, it wouldn't happen again. She kissed the mended picture and for a second time turned out the light.

She lay in the dark a while trying to think about the pony. But a curious thing happened: the image of the yellow cat trapped in the barbed wire kept pushing itself in front of the image of Tiny Joe. There were even times as she drifted off when she couldn't tell one from the other.

The next morning Lacey didn't have to be urged to get ready for school. She hurried, eager to hear from Rosette how the yellow cat was doing. Her father had gone to work early, so she and her mother ate breakfast by themselves.

"Nice people, the DiNallis, don't you think so?" said her mother as they drank their juice.

"Um hum," Lacey said, feeling hungrier than she had felt in a week, and helping herself to another piece of toast to prove it.

"Glad to see your appetite's returned, dear," said her mother. "Eat your toast, then run. Don't want you to be late."

As soon as she was ready Lacey kissed her mother and rushed off.

She didn't see Rosette in line on the playground, but when she walked into the classroom, Rosette and some of the other girls surrounded her.

"Tell them, Lacey," Rosette said. "Tell them what you did yesterday. And show them that terrible gash in your hand, too."

Lacey started to protest. The cut wasn't *that* bad. But she stopped herself and smiled at Rosette instead. Then she told the girls what had happened. They all stood quietly, their attention centered on her alone, the way the girls in Three Corners used to listen when she would talk about Tiny Joe. Soon the boys and Mrs. Klein came to listen, too.

"Wow!" said Willie Thompson after he had heard the story. "You took some chance, ole Lacey, the Lionhearted . . . trying to climb a ten-foot fence with barbed wire at the top. You know, some of those barbed wires give shocks." He winked. "And not corn shocks, either."

Lacey laughed. Willie Thompson would probably never let her live down that corn shock idea, but this morning she didn't even care.

"It was really Rosette's father who saved him," she said. "He's the one who got the cat breathing again after he had been choked."

"Oh, Rosette!" Mary grew wide-eyed. "How did your dad do that?"

Immediately all of them turned their attention from Lacey to Rosette. But Lacey didn't mind. They had listened to her for a little while. She had been a part of them for a little while and that was a start.

As she took her seat, she silently promised herself that she wouldn't talk so much about where she used to live, no matter how hard it was not to. She'd try to talk about things here and now. And maybe this week in gym class, she would turn the ropes the whole period without even taking a jump, if that's the way they did it here.

And . . . maybe . . . tonight after supper . . . she'd write Pam a letter and tell her all about Rosette and the yellow cat.